Emma Dilemma, the Nanny, and the Wedding

by Patricia Hermes

Amazon Children's Publishing

For Mark Joseph Hermes—at last!

Amazon Publishing
Attn: Amazon Children's Publishing
P.O. Box 400818
Las Vegas, NV 89149
www.amazon.com/amazonchildrenspublishing

Book design by Virginia Pope
Editor: Margery Cuyler

Printed in the United States of America (R)
First edition
10 9 8 7 6 5 4 3 2 1

Other **Emma Dilemma** books:

Dad

McClain

Annie

Emma

Lizzie + Ira

Tim

Mom

Contents

Chapter One
Emma Makes a Mess

Emma ran all the way home with a bunch of paint samples—little jars of different colors—jiggling in her pocket. All of them were Emma's favorite color—blue—brilliant blue, like her new soccer uniform. The paint store man had given them to her. Free! He said they were kind of old and maybe even dried out, and nobody wanted those bold colors anyway. Mom and Daddy said Emma could paint her room once she had decided on the color. First, she had wanted purple. Then she thought, *No, blue.* Electric blue.

Emma loved her room. She had a window seat with a fat, soft cushion, where she could sit and read and daydream and look out over the hills, all the way to the stable where her horse Rooney lived. She had bookcases and dollhouses, and for Christmas, Mom had said maybe she would get a

1

hanging chair. She had a ferret, Marmaduke, who she often set free to run around her room, and she even had her own special tree growing right outside her window.

Once inside the front door, Emma kicked off her shoes. The darkened hallway's long, polished floor called to her, perfect for sliding on in her sock feet.

Until two weeks ago, the hall had had deep red carpeting, nice and fuzzy on bare feet. But Mom decided it needed to be taken out because it had become so scuffed up and dirty. That was because of Woof, the family's huge, friendly poodle. Woof was always bringing in mud and leaves and sticks from rolling in the grass. Their cat, Kelley, brought in even nastier things, such as dead voles and mice. So some men came and pulled up the carpet and put down a new wood floor. Emma thought they made a bigger mess than any Woof and Kelley had ever made. Then Mom had told the men to put down new carpet in the family playroom, a pretty blue color, like early evening sky. Mom had frowned and sniffed, saying the new carpet smelled odd. After a day or two, though, she said it was okay.

It wasn't like Mom to be fussy or grumpy. But lately she seemed more tired than usual, maybe because of her work, which always made her grumpy. Mom worked for a museum in the city, though much of her work was done from home. Mom called it telecommuting. That's why Emma had gone to the paint store herself, without asking Mom to take her. The store was just a few blocks away, and Daddy said it was okay to go alone.

Whatever the reason for the new hall flooring, Emma loved it. She could slide really fast in sock feet, then pull up short, just before reaching the door to the playroom/family room where the family gathered. Now, she could hear talking inside; it sounded like McClain was giggling at something. McClain was Emma's five-year-old sister, sweet as anything, except when she had big temper tantrums, which were pretty frequent. Then it was best to leave her alone and not even look at her. If McClain was in there, then her cat, Kelley, was too. McClain dragged that cat around as if it were a stuffed toy. Kelley didn't seem to mind being squished up and dragged around. Emma also could hear Woof scrabbling. His collar clinked when he moved. But she didn't hear the twins, probably because they were napping.

And she'd bet anything that Tim, her big brother, was quiet because he was reading or studying maps with Daddy. Tim was a year older than Emma, but still, he worried about things that Emma never worried about. He worried that Daddy, who was a

3

pilot, would get lost in the sky. So Daddy always showed Tim his route before he took his next trip, because if Tim knew where Daddy was, he wouldn't worry as much. *Tim is the best brother in the whole world*, Emma thought. Worrying was the only thing he ever did wrong. He could get a gold medal for worrying!

It was good that the whole family was in the family room. Emma could show the paint jars to everyone and ask what they thought. Tim always had good ideas. Not Mom. If it were up to her, Emma's room would be plain, boring white.

Emma took a few steps, got a running start, and slid. She went so fast that when she got to the door at the end of the hall, she couldn't stop.

Bam! She fell and landed on her bottom, while her feet went out from under her and crashed into the door. As she went down, she banged her elbow on the floor really hard. The three jars of paint went skittering away from her.

"Emma! Is that you, honey?"

It was Mom calling from inside the playroom.

"It's me," Emma answered, sitting up and rubbing her elbow.

"Come in," Mom called. "We've been waiting for you. You weren't sliding down the hall again, were you?"

"Not really," Emma called. Then she added quietly, "Just a little."

Emma looked around for the paint jars. One jar had opened, and a tiny bit of paint had dribbled out and spotted the floor. Good. The paint hadn't dried up.

Emma rubbed at the paint dribble with her sock. The paint spot almost disappeared. But her sock got a little bit of blue on it. It didn't matter. It was on the bottom where nobody could see it.

Emma picked up all three jars and opened the door to the playroom.

The whole family was there—Mom, Daddy, Tim, McClain on the floor hugging Kelley, Woof, and the little twins, Ira and Lizzie. The twins were sound asleep on the couch, lying side by side, Lizzie with one finger in her mouth, Ira holding onto one of Lizzie's curls.

But where was Annie? And then Emma remembered—it was Saturday! Annie didn't work for them on Saturdays, although sometimes she stuck around because she wanted to be with them.

Emma loved Annie more than anything. Annie was the sweetest, funniest, kindest nanny in the whole world. Annie had her own apartment on the third floor of their house, and sometimes she even allowed Emma and the other kids to visit her up there at night—like if they got scared because of a thunderstorm or had trouble at school or with friends and were upset about something. It was like having your best friend living right in your house.

Annie also had a boyfriend, Bo. At first, Emma didn't like him much, but finally she'd gotten used to him.

When Emma came in, McClain popped up off the floor and ran to her. "Emma!" she cried, throwing herself against Emma and mashing Kelley between the two of them. "We've been waiting for you and waiting for you. Mom wants to tell us something important—a surprise, Mom said. But she wouldn't tell us till you got here."

Emma clutched the paint jars tight to her chest. "Stop it, McClain!" she said. "You're almost knocking me over."

"Mom?" McClain said. "Mom? Emma's here."

"Yes, McClain, I can see that," Mom answered.

"Then tell us!" McClain demanded.

McClain turned back to Emma. "What do you have there? It looks like paint. Is it paint? Can I see it, can it?" She tugged hard on Emma's arm again. The paint jars went tumbling down.

Paint dripped out—brilliant blue paint. It dripped on Emma's jeans. Onto McClain. Onto the new rug. And quite a lot of it onto Kelley.

Chapter Two

A New Baby

There was a lot of fuss and bother.

McClain began yelling at Kelley to stop licking the paint or she'd get poisoned.

Daddy hurried to the kitchen and got water and stuff. Then he went to work cleaning up the spot on the rug. He made little puffy sounds, as though he were working hard. Emma didn't see why spilling paint was such a big deal. The paint was blue and the rug was blue.

Emma took McClain by the arm and dragged her out to the kitchen. McClain held Kelley under one arm.

In the kitchen, McClain climbed up on the sink, took the sprayer, turned it on low, and sprayed it on Kelley's face. Kelley didn't fuss or yowl or anything. Then McClain opened Kelley's mouth wide and wiped the inside with her fingers. Even then, Kelley didn't fuss or try to bite or anything.

It made Emma wonder if Kelley were really a cat.

After a while, Emma and McClain got Kelley mostly clean, although her fur kind of stood up, stiff and patchy in places.

McClain tipped her head to one side. "Kelley looks like a porcupine, doesn't she?" she said.

"Yeah," Emma answered, "if God made blue ones."

"She's not that blue," McClain said. She went and got a big towel and wrapped Kelley in it. "Let's go," McClain said, heading back to the family room while carrying Kelley as if she were a fat little baby. "I want to hear what Mom and Daddy are going to tell us. I bet they're getting a divorce."

"What?" Emma said. "They'd never get a divorce."

"They had a fight before," McClain said.

In the family room, Emma sat down on the rug, and McClain sat beside her, still clutching Kelley. She bent her head near Emma's.

"Jasmine, in my kindergarten?" she said quietly. "Her parents got divorced and now she lives one week at her mom's and the other at her dad's. But her dad takes her to Disney World a lot. If Mom and Daddy get divorced, I bet Daddy will take us to Disney World too."

"McClain," Emma said quietly. "They are not getting divorced. They'd never do that."

"Okay, kids," Daddy said. "Can we settle down and talk now? And Emma, don't ever bring paint in here like that again. What were you thinking, carrying those jars without any lids on them?"

"The lids were there," Emma said. "But one lid fell off in the hall when I slipped."

"What?" Daddy said.

Emma nodded. "The man in the paint store gave me some samples. Free! I didn't even have to pay for them. And one is the color I wanted: electric blue. He said nobody liked these colors, and he'd had them for years, and they were probably all dried up anyway, but they're not because when I dropped the one in the hall—and that's how the top came off—some paint leaked out, so I knew it wasn't dried up and then . . . "

"Emma!" Mom said. "Where did you drop it? You didn't spill it on the new hall floor, did you? Is that the sound I heard in the hall?"

Emma turned to Mom. "No," she said. "Well . . . yes."

"What do you mean, no but yes?" Mom asked.

"Well, yes, I spilled it in the hall," Emma said. "But no, it's not spilled anymore because I wiped it up and it's all okay now."

"How did you wipe it up?" Mom asked.

"With my sock," Emma said. "There wasn't much."

Mom and Daddy exchanged looks.

"Really," Emma said. "It's all cleaned up. You can go look if you want. And the rug here looks okay."

Mom made a face.

"Mom, are you mad?" McClain asked.

Mom just shook her head. "No," she said, sighing. "Not mad."

"Are you still mad at Daddy?" McClain asked.

"At Daddy?" Mom said. "No. Why would I be mad at Daddy?"

McClain shrugged. "'Cause before, you wanted the crossword puzzle and Daddy said no."

Mom shook her head. Daddy did too. "Mom always wants it first," Daddy said. "But I'm better at it."

"Are not," Mom said. "You're just afraid I'll fill it all in."

"All right," Daddy said, looking across the room at Mom. "We've been bursting with some news for weeks. Shall we tell them?"

Mom straightened up and took a deep breath. "Yes," she said. "I'll tell."

Just then, the door banged open and Annie came flying in. She brought in cold air and she smelled of the outdoors, cold and fresh. "Hey, everyone," she said. "I have wonderful news."

The twins sat up, and Annie went to the couch and slid in between them, hugging their sleepy heads to her.

She frowned, then looked around. "Anything wrong?" she asked. "Why is everyone so serious?"

"Mom was mad at Daddy before," McClain said. "They're getting divorced. Probably."

"McClain!" Mom said. "What a dreadful thing to say. Of course we're not getting divorced."

"Well, you said it was big news," McClain said. She looked at Daddy. "Are you taking us to Disney World?"

Mom laughed. "No, McClain, we're not getting a divorce, and nobody's taking you to Disney World. It's big, happy news." Mom smiled at Daddy, then at Annie. "And Annie, I'm so glad you got here in time to hear the news too. We are having a baby. In a few months, there will be a new baby in the house."

"Cool!" Tim said.

"One baby or two?" Emma asked, remembering when the twins were born.

"We think one," Mom said. "But it's too early to tell for sure."

McClain made a face. "I'd rather go to Disney World," she said.

Chapter Three
Annie's Getting Married

After that, everybody started talking at once.

"What kind of baby?" McClain asked.

"We don't know yet," Mom said.

"I want a girl," McClain said.

"No!" Ira said. "A boy."

"When, when?" McClain said.

Emma looked at Tim. Tim was smiling, happy looking. He loved babies. He was still the best babysitter for the twins, and when the twins were little, he even changed their diapers.

Emma loved babies too—their softness and their sweet little fingers and toes. When the twins were little, she nibbled gently on their tiny toes, making them squirm and giggle. She didn't much like their diapers, though.

However, the one who seemed the most excited

and happy was Annie. She lifted the twins away from her and ran over to Mom.

Mom was flopped in the big lounge chair, her legs flung over the side. She looked as if she had no bones.

"Oh," Annie said, bending and putting her arms around Mom to hug her. "What a blessed gift." She kissed Mom on the forehead. Mom raised herself a little bit and hugged Annie back.

Next Annie crossed the room to Daddy. Emma wondered if Annie would kiss Daddy too. She didn't. She reached out to shake hands with him, which Emma thought was even weirder than kissing. Daddy stood up, laughing, and he hugged Annie. "We're so happy," he said.

"I am, too," Annie said, blushing a little bit, probably because of getting hugged. Then she went back to the sofa and pulled the twins to her again. They were yawning and rubbing their eyes.

"Now, Annie," Mom said. "You came in saying that you had wonderful news?"

"Well," Annie said. "Yes. I . . . well, I'm excited too."

"What?" McClain said. "Tell us!"

"Calm down, McClain," Daddy said. "Let Annie take her time."

Annie laughed. She looked up. "I'm getting married!" she said.

"You are?" Mom said. "Oh, my goodness, that is wonderful news. Congratulations, Annie."

"And soon," Annie said.

"When?" Tim asked. He sounded worried.

"Married?" Lizzie asked.

"That's when you get to live with somebody," Ira said. "Like Mom and Daddy, right?"

"Right," McClain said. "And then you get lots of kids and a dog. And a cat. And maybe a ferret, though maybe not."

"Children," Daddy said. "Could we let Annie talk, please?" He turned to Annie. "What are your wedding plans?"

"We don't have any yet," Annie said. "We just decided this morning."

Emma's heart started leaping around inside her. "Are you going to leave us?" she asked.

"Oh, no," Annie said. "I'm going to stay right here with you, my dears. It seems your mom might need my help even more after the baby comes."

"But where will Bo live?" Emma asked. "I mean, where will you and Bo live?"

"I told you, just this morning we decided to get married. So we haven't had time to think about it."

"Well, *think*," Emma said.

"Here!" Lizzie said. "Annie lives here."

"With us!" Ira said.

14

"You know you're both welcome to keep right on living up in your apartment," Mom said.

Annie smiled. "Thank you," she said. "We'll think about it. But we might move to Bo's since it's closer to his school."

Annie held out her hand, looking down at it dreamily.

"Oh!" Mom said. "A ring. May I see it?"

Mom sat up straighter, and Annie went over to her, first moving the twins back to the sofa.

"It's beautiful!" Mom said, sucking in her breath. "Oh, my goodness! An emerald."

"Green. Because of Ireland," Annie said.

"I don't think you should move to Bo's place," Emma said. "I really don't think that's a good idea."

"Emma," Daddy said. "Annie and Bo will decide in their own time. Let's leave Annie be for now."

"I'm not leaving you," Annie said, coming and sitting on the floor beside Emma. "I've told you that a zillion times. No matter where we live, I'll be here every day. Just like always."

Emma took Annie's hand. She looked down at Annie's ring. It sparkled up at her.

Emma turned to Tim.

Tim was scowling. Emma knew why—for the same reason Emma was.

"But what about nighttime?" Emma whispered,

turning back to Annie, still holding her hand.

"Don't fret, me dear," Annie said, just as softly. "We'll work things out."

Emma breathed in deep. "How?"

Annie didn't answer. She just kept smiling down at the sparkly ring on her hand, looking as if she were already somewhere else.

Chapter Four

Too Many Changes

After a minute, Daddy spoke. "Annie, so you have no definite plans, not even a date yet?"

Annie shook her head. "No. We haven't even thought about it. As I said, we only decided this very morning, when Bo gave me the ring. I was thinking of having the wedding in Ireland, because my family's there. But then I thought that might not be fair to Bo because his family is *here*."

Don't go back to Ireland, Emma thought.

"The only thing is," Annie went on, "we have to get married during Bo's school break. That will be around the holidays, Christmastime, probably."

"Christmas is soon!" Tim said.

"Right," Annie answered. "In just a few weeks. That's when Bo's school break is. And then—now I'm just thinking out loud, because as I said, we haven't decided anything—maybe even me sisters could come from Ireland if they could afford to, and if they could get the time off. You know they teach, and schools close for Christmas holidays."

"Maybe that can be our wedding present to you, Annie," Daddy said. "My airline could arrange flights for your sisters, flights that wouldn't cost too much. There's something called 'friends and families' flights' that are cheap."

"I know what!" Emma said, hugging Annie's hand tightly. "Here. Have the wedding here." She turned to Mom. "Oh, can we, can we, Mom and Daddy? Can we? And all the sisters can come here?"

Then Annie won't go and be gone a long time.

"Oh!" Mom said, straightening up in her chair. "What a lovely idea, Emma." Mom looked over at Daddy. "Shall we do that? Have the wedding here? Annie's sisters can stay here too."

Daddy smiled and nodded. "I think our house is big enough," he said. "And it will be all decorated for Christmas— it would be lovely."

"Oh, yippee!" McClain said. "I'm going to be the flower girl! Can I, Annie? Can I?"

"No, McClain!" Emma said. "I asked to have the wedding here, so I should have the first choice."

"But I asked for flower girl first," McClain said.

"Me!" Ira said.

"You can't be a *flower girl*. You're a boy," McClain said.

Ira howled. "Not fair!"

"It's okay. We'll fix it," Lizzie said to Ira, though how and what she'd "fix," Emma had no idea.

"Children, please!" Mom said. "Manners, please."

The twins leaned their heads together, whispering to one another. Emma figured they were planning their own rebellion.

"Annie?" Emma said, as softly and politely as she could. "Can I be in your wedding too? Please? May I?"

"Of course," Annie said. "Why, if we have the wedding here, you can all be in it. Every single one of you." She turned to Daddy. "Oh, this will be such fun. Thank you so much for offering. But are you sure?" Annie turned from Daddy to Mom. "It seems like a lot of money. And work. Especially with a new baby on the way."

"Not work at all," Mom said. "Well, work, yes, but happy work. Just like a new baby. Lots of work, but so much joy."

Daddy looked at the big clock over the mantle. "Okay, kiddos," he said. "It's after five. I vote for dinner."

"I vote pizza!" McClain said, jumping up and

dumping Kelley off her lap. Kelley sure looked weird, not like a cat at all. Or even a blue porcupine. More like a blue creature from a cartoon.

Daddy laughed. "Nobody said we were taking votes."

"Did too," McClain said. "You voted for dinner."

"I vote hot dogs," Lizzie said, scrambling off the couch.

"Me too," Ira said, tumbling after her.

Woof jumped up and started to lead them out of the playroom.

At the door, McClain stopped, one hand on Woof's head. She turned around. "Are hot dogs made from dogs?" she asked.

"No. They are not made out of dogs," Mom said, laughing. She reached out for McClain and pulled her into a hug.

"Then why do we call them 'dogs'?" McClain asked.

"I don't know," Mom said. "That's a good question."

"So we could call them 'hot cats' if we wanted, right?"

"I guess we could," Mom said, laughing again.

McClain nodded. "Yup. But you can't put cats in the microwave."

She thought for a minute more, and then added, "Dogs either."

Again Mom laughed.

"Let's forget hot dogs and hot cats," Daddy said. "Mom's had a nice stew simmering on the stove all day. Can you smell it? It's going to be heavenly."

McClain wrinkled up her nose. "Hate stew," she muttered.

Mom turned and went to her desk for a notebook. Emma knew why. Mom was going to make lists.

Mom loved lists.

Emma liked to write in her notebook, too, but not lists. She liked her secret book that was like a diary, except it wasn't exactly. It was just for writing about stuff she liked. And hated. And wanted. What would she write tonight?

She didn't want Annie to get married. But she did want to be in a wedding. She'd get to meet Annie's sisters—her seven sisters from Ireland. She'd already talked to them on the phone a few times. And they were funny; they always made her laugh. And, oh, she'd probably get a new dress. She wanted a long one, one that went all the way to the floor.

There were so many things happening. New things. Wonderful things.

And some not-so-wonderful things.

There would be a sweet new baby.

But . . . even sweet babies cried at night.

And Annie would be married. And she might not be at the house at night! She might be at Bo's.

Emma sighed. She thought she might *not* like all that was happening. Not all of the changes anyway.

Chapter Five
Crazy Wild Dinnertime

Annie didn't always eat with the family, only sometimes. But Mom had asked her to stay so that they could celebrate all the good news together.

Annie sat across the table from Emma, with Lizzie on one side of her and Ira on the other. The minute they sat down, Lizzie threw her arms around Annie's neck, hugging her tight. Lizzie was always hugging Annie. But now it seemed that she was hugging Annie so hard, Annie could hardly move, much less breathe.

"I love you," Lizzie said.

"Me too," Ira said.

"Annie?" McClain said, "Annie?"

Annie didn't answer right away. She was busy trying to unwrap Lizzie's arms from around her neck. "You trying to choke me before I get married?" Annie said.

"Annie!" McClain said again. "Annie, I'm trying to talk to you."

"Children, take it easy," Daddy said. "Annie is just one person. Give her time."

"And space," Mom said softly.

"Annie?" McClain said. "Annie, I have to ask you something."

"All right," Annie said, untwisting Lizzie's arms and kissing the top of her head. "What is it, McClain? Do you want to tell me you love me, too?"

"No," McClain said. "Well, yes. But when you get married, you have to love your husband best, right? That's the rule, isn't it?"

"No," Annie answered. "You just make room in your heart for more people. I can love you *and* I can love Bo. Just like your mom can love all of you *and* the new baby too."

""Oh," McClain said. "Like the Grinch."

"The *Grinch*?" Mom said. "Well, I hope not."

McClain turned to Mom. "You have to watch the movie all the way till the end. At the end, his heart swells up so much that he can love. It gets very big. Supersize."

"Oh," Mom said.

"So I can love you and Bo and your new baby too," Annie said.

"But you still might move away," McClain said.

24

Once more, Lizzie threw her arms around Annie's neck.

"Don't go! Don't go!" she cried.

Ira reached across and tried hugging Annie too. "Don't!" he said. "Don't go!"

And in the reaching and hugging, the water pitcher got knocked over. Water spilled everywhere—on the tablecloth, onto the twins and the table, and onto Emma and McClain.

Emma and McClain both pushed themselves away from the table and jumped up. The water ran down Emma's legs. It was cold!

Annie and Tim headed quickly for the kitchen to get towels to clean up the mess.

Ira, who, besides Tim, was the sweetest boy on the face of the earth, reached over and pinched Lizzie's arm! "Your fault!" he said.

Lizzie pinched Ira back, and then Ira started howling. They plopped back down in their chairs and leaned their heads together, as if they were best friends and hadn't just pinched one another.

Daddy got up and tried to help. He lifted the bread basket off the soaked tablecloth. He said, "It's all right, it's all right, it's just a bit of water."

Tim and Annie came back into the dining room with towels and began wiping things up. Tim said the same thing as Daddy. "It's all right, it's all right.

It's just water." Daddy sounded calm, soothing. Tim didn't.

"Please stop *yelling!*" Tim said.

Annie picked up the twins, tucking one under each arm. They had grown so big that their arms and legs dangled every which way.

But they finally stopped screaming. Annie wiped up the booster seats that were swimming in water.

"There now, there now," Annie murmured.

"Ira pinched me," Lizzie said, her bottom lip thrust out.

"You pinched first," Ira said.

"Did not!" Lizzie said. "*You* did."

Which, of course, he had.

Emma turned to Mom. Mom had closed her eyes, the way she did when she was really upset. She called it "being at the end of my wits." Emma didn't know what "wits" had to do with it, but she did know "upset" when she saw it.

Once the water had dried up and the twins had stopped howling, Daddy served the stew. It was mostly vegetables, and Emma actually liked vegetables, even cooked ones. But she despised and detested cooked tomatoes. This stew was swimming in them. The skins slid off, and the insides were slimy. Emma shuddered.

Beside Emma, McClain made a nasty face. She

leaned close to Emma. "Remember that raccoon?" she whispered.

Emma frowned. "Raccoon?"

"You know!" McClain said. "The one that got run over in front of our house that time? And its guts were all over the place?"

"Ick," Emma said, remembering. "And Kelley ate it."

McClain nodded and looked down at her bowl of stew. "Gut stew," she whispered.

Daddy had handed around the bowls, and Mom was passing a loaf of French bread. With butter. Emma helped herself to a piece of bread and a big lot of butter. To Emma, butter was the only reason to eat bread. Also, if she filled up on bread, she wouldn't need to eat the gut stew.

When everyone was served, Daddy asked his usual question: Who wants to say the blessing?

Nobody offered.

Daddy looked around the table. "Nobody?" he asked.

Both Ira and Lizzie still looked teary. Lizzie had jutted out her bottom lip as if she were ready to howl again at any moment.

Emma didn't feel like praying.

"Okay, I will," McClain said.

"No!" Tim said. "I will."

Emma knew why Tim spoke up. McClain's prayers went on and on. She prayed for everything. Last night, she had even prayed for the sugar bowl.

"Go ahead, Tim," Daddy said.

"But I wanted to say thank you for our new baby!" McClain said. "And for Annie's new baby that she'll have soon. . . . "

"McClain!" Daddy said.

"What?" McClain said. "That's what happens when people get married."

"Not always," Daddy said.

"And not right away," Annie said. She had a stern look on her face, but Emma could tell that she was trying hard not to laugh.

"McClain," Daddy said. "Please don't say inappropriate things. And Tim, would you go on with the blessing? Maybe a thank you for our new baby? And for Annie's happiness with Bo?"

Tim took a deep breath. He bent over his folded hands. "We are thankful for our new baby." He paused a moment. Then he added, "And thankful that Annie is happy and is getting married. Amen."

Everyone said "Amen," and then Mom said, "Tim, that's very sweet."

Tim raised his head. He looked at Emma. Emma could tell that Tim wasn't being sweet and that he wasn't thankful at all for Annie getting married.

Emma thought his prayer was the first bad thing he had ever said in his whole, entire life. He had just told a big, fat lie.

To God!

Chapter Six
Middle-of-the-Night Plan

After dinner, Emma ran upstairs. She had to let Marmaduke out of his cage so he could run around. Ferrets need a lot of exercise and he'd been closed up all day.

Woof followed Emma into her room. Emma took Marmaduke out of his cage. She held him to her face the way she always did, asking for a kiss. Marmaduke stuck his furry, cute face right up to Emma's, right against her lips.

Emma held Marmaduke's face up to Woof. Marmaduke gave Woof a kiss too. Woof shook his big head and buried his face in his paws as if he were shaking off the kiss.

Marmaduke squirmed and turned in Emma's arms, fussing to get down. She set him on the floor. Right away, he started running around the room, up across the desk, down onto the rug, up to the window seat, and round and round. Woof ran after him.

They bumped into furniture, leaped on and off the bed, and made a big racket and mess. Finally, Marmaduke shot up to the very top of Emma's bookshelves. He crouched and panted, grinning down at Woof. *Ha!* he seemed to say. *Try and catch me now!*

Woof chose to ignore him. He leapt onto Emma's bed and turned in a circle before settling in. *I am not interested in chasing you any longer*, he told Marmaduke, very formally.

Emma plopped down beside Woof on the bed and put her arms around him. She also kept one eye on Marmaduke. She had to watch him carefully when he was free. The windows and door were closed tightly, but Emma knew that if there were even a crack, he'd run out. One terrible time, he had escaped from the house. It had been raining and it was dark out, and Emma had been scared they'd never find him. But Bo found Marmaduke and brought him home. Marmaduke was wet and dirty and looked a little bit like a rat. That's when Emma had first decided that Bo was okay, although before she hadn't been so sure.

Now, there was a knock on Emma's door. Tim. Had to be.

"Come on in, Tim," she called out, "but shut the door quick. Marmaduke's loose."

Tim came in, closing the door quickly behind him. He sat on the edge of the bed. "How'd you know it was me?" he asked.

"Because you're the only one in the family who obeys the house rule—that nobody can go into anybody else's room without knocking. The little kids forget. And McClain just doesn't bother."

"You should be a detective," Tim said.

Marmaduke came to check him out, creeping out from under the bed. He nibbled on Tim's socks and Tim jumped.

"How'd you get down there?" Emma said.

"Where?" Tim asked.

"I wasn't talking to *you*," Emma said. "I was talking to Marmaduke. A second ago, he was on top of the bookcase."

"Oh!" Tim said. He picked up Marmaduke and held him against his chest. Marmaduke started to dig his way under Tim's shirt. He loved burying himself inside things, anything snug and hidden.

"Emma," Tim said, stroking Marmaduke through his shirt, "Are you worried?"

Emma nodded. "You?"

Tim nodded. "Yeah. Annie's going to move to Bo's place. I'm sure of it."

"But maybe not," Emma said. "She's told us a gazillion times that she loves us and will be our nanny forever or until we don't need her anymore. Besides, it will be fun to be in a wedding."

Tim made a face. "That's just because you're a girl," he said. "She didn't promise not to *move*. What if she goes to live in Bo's apartment? What about thunderstorms? Then what?"

Emma sighed. "I know," she said. Tim wasn't just scared of thunderstorms. He was terrified. Sometimes he even went into a closet and closed the door and stayed there till the storm was over. And he was ten years old!

Emma chewed on the inside of her lip for a while.

"Well, why wouldn't she stay?" Emma asked at last, more to make Tim feel better than because she believed what she was about to say. "She has a whole apartment upstairs, with a big living room and a big bedroom and a kitchen and a bathroom and she loves having Woof and Kelley and Marmaduke visit her. And us kids when we need her, and . . ."

"Nope!" Tim interrupted. "Even if she stays, she might not want us to visit anymore."

"What are you talking about?" Emma said. "Why wouldn't she?"

Tim shrugged. "Guys change when they get married. Like, I bet Daddy was a lot of fun once."

"Daddy's nice!" Emma said.

"I know!" Tim said. "But I bet if he and Mom were just married, and suddenly Mom's family arrived with a whole bunch of kids and a dog and cat and ferrets . . . "

"*One* ferret," Emma said.

"*One* ferret," Tim said. "I bet Daddy wouldn't be happy. He'd want his own apartment without all those animals and people. Just him and Mom."

Emma frowned. She hadn't thought of that. How awful! Could that really happen—would Bo not want them up in Annie's apartment? Emma wasn't scared about thunderstorms, not the way Tim was. But she had other worries that she could tell Annie only in private. There was that time she had stolen a book—not exactly stolen it but more borrowed it without permission—and was going to give it back the very next day after she had read it. But she fell asleep reading, and while she slept, Marmaduke chewed the book into little pieces. That was the kind of thing Annie could help with, as she had done that time.

"Well," Emma said after a minute, "why don't we ask her? Why don't we just say: 'Are you or aren't you going to stay with us? And if you stay, can we still come talk to you at night? Or on Saturdays? Or any time we need to?' Annie will tell us the truth.

She always does. Even better," Emma said, sitting up. "You're the one worrying, so *you* ask her."

For some reason, Emma couldn't admit that she was worried too.

"I can't," Tim said.

"Why not?" asked Emma.

"Because what if she says yes, she's moving?" Tim said. "Or what if she says she's staying, but we're not welcome to visit her anymore and . . ."

Emma closed her eyes, just like Mom did when she was at the end of her wits. Emma didn't *feel* at the end of her wits, just kind of annoyed with Tim.

"Okay," Emma said, taking a deep breath and trying to sound very reasonable, like Mom. "What if Annie says no, she's *not* moving? And yes, we can visit her? Then you'll feel happy and you can stop worrying and go to sleep, right?"

"She's not going to say that," Tim said.

Again, Emma closed her eyes. She sighed.

"Children! Tim? Emma? Have you two had your baths or showers yet?"

It was Mom calling. "It's almost bedtime."

Tim stood up. He opened Emma's door. "Coming!" he called. "How about we *both* ask her?" Tim said, turning back to Emma. "Together!"

"But not till late. When everybody's asleep."

That was because the kids weren't even allowed

35

to call Annie on her phone at night. But if they were very, very quiet, and softly opened Annie's door, Annie almost always heard them and said, "Come on up, me dears! Whoever you are."

Tim very gently shook Marmaduke from his shirt, lowering him to the floor.

Emma bent to pick him up. Before she could get her hands on him, though, he was out the door, scooting across the hall and down the stairs.

Emma flew after him. She tumbled down a few steps and grabbed him, landing on her belly—and on Marmaduke.

"Oh, no you don't, little buddy," she said. "You're staying right here with me."

She carried Marmaduke back to her room, closed the door, and set him on the bed, frowning at him.

Right away, Marmaduke scampered off the bed and up to the very top of her bookcase. He sat there, frowning down at her.

Emma's door opened. Tim. This time, he didn't knock. "Are you going to stay awake?" he asked.

"I'll try," Emma said.

"You'll wake me up?"

Emma nodded.

"Okay," Tim said, "but don't scare me."

"I never scare you," Emma said.

"Once you did," Tim said.

Emma made a face at him. "Go!" she said. "Go have your shower. I'll wake you later."

Which she did.

"And I won't scare you," she said.

Which she didn't.

Chapter Seven
Annie Might Move!

It was a few minutes after midnight. All the lights were out. The little kids had gone to sleep. McClain had stopped singing to her dolls. Marmaduke was asleep in his cage. No light was shining from under Mom and Daddy's door. The TV wasn't on.

The whole house was sleeping.

All but Emma and Tim. And Woof who had to be in on everything. The three of them stood at the far end of the hall by the door to Annie's apartment. Emma was wearing her favorite froggie slippers. She had had a hard time waking Tim without scaring him. Eventually, she remembered something that had worked before—she blew on his face. He wiped his hand across it in his sleep, as if something were tickling him, and finally woke up. Even so, it took him ages to get on his robe and tie it, and get his flashlight and test that it was working, and by then, Emma was totally annoyed with him.

When Tim finally got himself together, they went and stood in front of Annie's apartment door. A light was shining under the bottom crack, so Emma knew Annie was awake.

Carefully, quietly, Emma turned the door handle and opened the door just a crack. "Annie?" she whispered.

No answer.

She said it just a tiny bit louder. She wouldn't go up without being invited. "Annie?" she called again.

Woof didn't care about being invited. He had no manners at all. He pushed the door wide and went galumphing up the stairs, the tags on his collar jingling.

"Well, look who's here!" Emma heard Annie say. "And who's with you?"

"It's me!" Emma answered softly. "Me, Emma."

"Me, Tim," Tim said.

"Well, come up here, me darlings," Annie called. She used that sweet voice that she used sometimes. She called it her Irish voice. Mom said it was a lilting voice. It sounded almost like singing.

They both scrambled up the stairs and into Annie's big apartment. Annie was sitting on the floor by the wide windows. Wedding magazines were spread out around her, spilling off the table and piled up on her lap.

She pushed them away and held out both arms. "Come to me, you rascals," she said. "What are you doing up so late? Sure, don't you know the fairies are about this time of night?"

Emma screwed up her face. "I don't believe in fairies," she said.

"Silly thing to say!" Annie said, pretending to be horrified. "Ooh, they will catch you up if they hear you say that. Come here now!"

Emma ran into Annie's arms, but Tim held back. He was shy about being hugged, although usually after a while he gave in.

"Tim was worried," Emma said, curling up in Annie's arms. Under her breath, she added, kind of quietly, "I was too."

"You were worried too," Tim said, sounding mad.

Emma shrugged. "That's what I said!" she said.

"Worried about what?" Annie asked. She settled Emma on her lap, shifting around so the magazines were out of the way.

Emma looked over at Tim. "Go ahead," Emma said. "Ask. See what she says."

Tim plopped down on the floor and pulled Woof

into his arms. He buried his face in Woof's neck.

"Ask me what?" Annie asked.

Tim said something, but with his face buried in Woof's fur, it sounded as if he said "humph, humph, bo, bluggle, humph, humph."

"What was that?" Annie said.

"Okay," Emma said. "I'll do it. Annie, after you get married, will you still live with us? You and Bo both? I know you said maybe. But Tim said you . . . well, you wouldn't want us up here with you, even if you did stay. Because you'd be married." For some reason, Emma couldn't add that Bo wouldn't want them.

"Oh, me dear," Annie said. She spoke into Emma's hair. "I'll be with you till you don't need me anymore, I've told you that. You're my family. That isn't going to change because I get married."

"I know," Emma said, pulling away a little from Annie and sitting up straight.

Annie sighed. "You don't leave your family, not in your heart," she said. "But sometimes you have to move away. Just as I had to leave my beloved sisters and mum in Ireland to come here to get a job."

"But you don't have to do that now," Emma said, "because you have a job. Taking care of us. Right?"

"Right," Annie said. "But Bo doesn't have a job.

He's in graduate school, and we have to be near his school, especially during the bad weather, because of snow. See, we need to be sure he can get to his classes."

"Schools close when it's snowing hard," Emma said.

"Children's schools close," Annie said, "if the snow is really deep. But that's not true for big people's schools. Like colleges. And graduate schools. They usually stay open. Unless there's a blizzard or something."

"So?" Emma said. A bad feeling had begun growing inside her, and her heart was beating fast. She swallowed back tears. Annie was going to leave them!

"Bo's apartment is close to his school," Annie went on. "He can walk there if he has to. From here, it would be hard. You know that your house is in a hollow, where you can slide down the hills in the snow. And don't you remember how there were times when your daddy couldn't get his car up the hill?"

Emma turned to Tim. He had that look on his face, the I-told-you-so look.

"So," Emma said, trying to sound very reasonable, and fighting back the tears, "when we know a snowstorm is coming, then you can go to

Bo's apartment. I'll help you pack up your stuff, coats and sweaters and your big snow boots too. Or even better! I have an idea. You stay here, and Bo can go to his apartment. That way, you're here. With us! And Bo's close to school!"

Annie squeezed Emma to her. "I don't think it's that simple, sweetie. I think it would be better to set up housekeeping in one place."

"Then you *are* moving to Bo's place?" Emma's voice came out harsh sounding, as if her throat were being squeezed by a big hand. It was what happened when she was trying to talk and not cry at the same time.

"*Ours*," Annie said. "It will be *our* house, wherever we settle. But we haven't decided anything, really. And even if we do move to Bo's apartment, it won't be any different for you, my dears. I will drive over here in the mornings. Only instead of coming downstairs, I'll be coming from my car. It will be just as it always is."

No, Emma thought. *It won't be. Because even now, it isn't the same. Not at all. Not inside my heart.*

Chapter Eight

Emma Is Mad. Tim Is, Too.
So Is Woof.

Everybody was quiet for a few minutes. The only sound was Woof's jingling collar as he scratched himself.

Emma couldn't speak. Tears welled up in her eyes. She blinked hard to keep them from spilling over.

Annie turned to Tim. "Come here, Tim," she said. "Bring that big beast with you."

Both Woof and Tim got up. They settled down on the other side of Annie, but far enough away from her so that she couldn't reach out and hug them. After a minute, though, Woof broke free from Tim's grasp and snuggled right in close to Annie, sticking his furry head on her lap. Annie ruffled up his ears.

Emma straightened up and looked around at all of Annie's things. This room would be terrible without Annie in it. Pictures of Annie's family were on the table, all of her sisters smiling out at them. Now there wouldn't be any more pictures, or any of Annie's books or her pretty clothes or her guitar—or anything!

Annie had even put a big lace "thing" over her bed, like a canopy or something, and it drifted down, making the bed look as if it belonged to a princess. And in the summer, when the windows were open, the canopy blew a little in the breeze.

In the big room, where they were sitting now, Annie had attached tiny bells to her curtains, and they tingled when the curtains moved.

Emma thought this was the prettiest room and apartment *ever*. But with Annie gone, everything would be different.

Emma blinked hard again. *She would not cry!*

She pulled farther away from Annie, got up, and wandered over to the table. She looked down at the pictures that Annie's sisters sent every month.

There were also pictures of Bo. Some of the pictures looked new. They weren't yet in frames or anything; they were just lying there. Emma picked up one of the pictures of Bo. She looked at him for a minute. He was kind of good looking, but with weird yellow hair that stood up every which way. She put his picture back on the table.

Face down. She picked up one of the photos of the seven sisters too. They were beautiful, every one of them. Emma sighed. She'd love to meet them. If only it wasn't at a wedding—at Annie's wedding.

For some reason, Emma wanted the picture of the sisters. She wanted to just look at them for a while. She could have asked. Annie would probably have said yes. But Emma didn't ask. Instead, she put the picture in her pajama pocket and walked back to where Annie was sitting. She plopped down on the rug, making sure to have an innocent look on her face.

"Is this why all my darlings seemed upset at dinnertime?" Annie asked. "Just because of me moving, because I *might* move?"

"It wasn't just us kids," Emma said. "Mom and Daddy were worried too!"

"Oh, maybe, but not about me moving," Annie said, laughing. "They have a lot on their minds. They are being so kind to have the wedding at this house. Your mum will get flowers and food and things to drink. It's going to be a big party. I called me sisters and mum. They're so excited. They'll all be coming! I talked to your daddy after supper, and he's already arranging flights for them and . . ."

"Wait!" Emma interrupted. "You told us once

that airline tickets cost a lot of money, so they probably won't come. So maybe you should get married some other time. Not now."

Annie laughed again. It seemed that no matter what Emma said, Annie laughed.

"Oh, don't you worry," Annie said. "Remember? Your daddy said he might be able to get some inexpensive flights for them because of being a pilot for the airlines. And he said he might hire a limousine to bring them from the airport to here. Because there will be eight of them and luggage, and that means they won't fit in your cars. But he'll get a long limo, and oh, they've never been in a limousine before and they'll be so excited. I'll keep that a secret. After they land, they'll be so surprised to see that big, long shiny car waiting just for them." Annie clapped her hands. "Doesn't that sound like fun? Like a wonderful surprise? They'll feel like Cinderella."

Emma shrugged. She didn't see why a limo was such a big deal. Unless a movie star was in it.

"And we'll have a big wedding cake," Annie went on. "Me sister Bridget is really good at baking and decorating cakes, and she can make the prettiest cake you can imagine. It'll be so pretty you won't even want to cut into it. Emma, I know you like banana flavor. That would be nice, wouldn't it?"

47

"What if there's a thunder and lightning storm?" Emma said.

"At my wedding? We don't have thunderstorms in winter. Not usually, anyway."

"No!" Emma said. "I meant any time. Here. Like, you know, like always. We come up here and snuggle with you when we're scared. Or worried. Like tonight. But if you're not here, then we can't come up and snuggle with you and get over being worried."

"Or scared," Tim added.

"Oh, I see," Annie said slowly. "I'm afraid I didn't think about that."

"Well, *think* about it!" Emma said. She knew she sounded mean, but she couldn't help it. "Up here is where we go to be . . . to be not scared."

"Emma dear, we haven't decided *definitely* on Bo's place yet," Annie said, quietly. "We're still working on things. Besides, if we do decide to live at his apartment, I'll only be a mile away."

"Right!" Emma said. "And I suppose you want us to run the mile in the dark in my froggie slippers and my rain coat, and . . . "

" . . . and carrying a flashlight," Tim added.

Emma made a face at him. "And carrying a flashlight, and getting all wet and maybe even getting *struck by lightning*."

"No," Annie said. "No, no, no. But maybe you're big enough now so that you don't need cuddling in a thunderstorm." She looked at Tim.

"Stupid," Tim said.

Emma nodded.

It was stupid—really, really stupid. Tim would never get over being afraid of thunderstorms. Emma wasn't really scared of storms. But she thought of all the other times she had needed Annie. Times like tonight. Only tonight, Annie wasn't making things better at all.

All she was doing was laughing. And not thinking about how Emma felt.

Emma stood up.

Tim raised his eyebrows at her.

She nodded and he stood up too.

So did Woof, shaking himself free of Annie. Woof looked from Tim to Emma, then back to Annie.

"Well," Emma said, pushing her fists down on her hips. "Goodnight then!" She used her meanest, maddest voice.

"Goodnight then," Tim said, mad and mean sounding too. He didn't sound as angry as Emma, though, probably because he hadn't had as much practice.

Woof looked up at Emma.

Emma had this queer feeling that Woof was

about to say "goodnight then!" also, sounding just as mad and mean as they did.

He didn't.

Emma grabbed his collar. "Come on!" she said. And all three of them went stomping down the stairs.

And then, very softly, in that sweet Irish voice, that lilting voice, Annie called after them, "Good night, me dears."

Emma just hated it when Annie did stuff like that.

Chapter Nine
Marmaduke Hides Out

When Emma awoke, it was still dark out. Something had awakened her. She lay still, wondering. Was it Marmaduke? Was he creeping around her bed?

No. It wasn't Marmaduke. It was an idea. The idea had awakened her.

Emma sat up. Measles! She could get measles. She had heard that you were sick for weeks with measles. If she was really sick, Annie wouldn't marry and leave. Annie fussed and fussed over the kids when they were sick. She fussed even more than Mom and Daddy did—and Daddy fussed like anything. Annie was always tiptoeing into their rooms to check on them at night.

No. Wouldn't work. Emma had had a measles shot so she couldn't get measles. Besides, she wouldn't know how to go about getting them.

Emma lay back and closed her eyes. She turned on her side, then her back, then her other side. But sleep had gone.

She could feel the sisters' photo in her pajama pocket. She opened her eyes. She took the photo out and studied it. They were all so pretty. And they all looked like Annie! She couldn't wait to meet them. If only Annie weren't getting married.

What if Emma broke her arm? No.

What if she got poison ivy? She had had that once. It had covered her whole body. It had made her feel awful.

No, she didn't want to do that again.

Oh! What if Annie got poison ivy?

Even better —what if Bo got poison ivy? They couldn't have a wedding if the groom was covered with poison ivy!

Emma had read once that if you rubbed poison ivy on someone's bed sheets, they'd get poison ivy all over their body. Or if you rubbed it on their clothing . . .

It was becoming a tiny bit lighter in the room. Birds were beginning to hop around in the tree outside, announcing morning was on its way. Even though it was winter, the birds still hopped around outdoors. Emma wondered if they were cold, with only their little feathers to keep them warm. She hoped not. Once, she had opened the window to let them in during a snowstorm. But even though they were shivering, they wouldn't come in.

Emma slid out of bed. She went to Marmaduke's cage. He was sitting up, blinking, the way he did when he first woke up. He bounced around, happy to see her.

Emma opened the cage and lifted him out, hugging him to her. He was warm and snuggly.

She brought him over to the window seat, her favorite place for sitting and thinking. She sat pondering the tree that that horrible man in Maine had planted for her. His name was Mr. Thompson and although he was horrible, he had wanted her to have a new tree to make up for his cutting down Emma's favorite tree in Maine. She still missed the other tree, though it did make her happy to have her very own tree outside her window, giving the birds places to huddle against the cold. The only problem was that this tree was young, so it was kind of skinny. The Maine tree had been huge, hundreds of years old. Emma would be three hundred years old before her new tree got that big.

"Marmaduke," Emma whispered. "Are you sad that Annie's going to leave us?"

Marmaduke rubbed his head up and down Emma's cheek. It was his way of saying, yes, it was awful for her to leave.

"Are you happy about New Baby?"

Marmaduke just looked at Emma. He didn't seem to have any feelings about that.

"Do you have any ideas for how to keep Annie here?"

Marmaduke rested his head against Emma's shoulder. He sighed. Emma knew what that meant—no ideas.

"You don't think poison ivy is a good idea, do you?"

Marmaduke actually pulled away and stared at her. His face looked very stern.

"Well, I didn't say I'd do it!" Emma said. "I was just thinking about it."

Marmaduke kept staring.

Emma plopped him down, sort of hard.

She thought some more. No, it was totally awful what she'd been thinking. She'd never do something so bad. She felt terrible and mean. But she reminded herself that thinking something bad wasn't the same as *doing* something bad. Daddy had told her that a thousand times when she had been thinking bad things about Mr. Thompson when he cut down her tree in Maine.

And then Emma remembered something important: her magic ball. She had had it for ages. If you asked it questions, it gave you answers. She'd ask it now and see what happened.

She jumped down from the window seat, went to her desk, and opened the top drawer. There was a mess of stuff inside, crayons and broken pencils and hair clips. But the crystal ball was there, too, buried right in the mess. There was also the instruction book that came with it that explained how it could answer your questions about the future, and a fat booklet that said, "Amazing magic tricks to astound your family and friends."

Emma picked up the crystal ball. It wasn't really crystal, just some kind of black plastic. You asked it questions, then turned it this way and that, and an answer floated up from inside to the top. Emma didn't believe that it really knew the answers. It was so random. Still, she couldn't resist.

She took the ball and went and sat on her window seat. "Can I keep Annie here?" she asked.

She tilted the ball this way and that. The answer floated up. "Probably not," it said.

Emma let out her breath. Stupid! She'd ask it in a different way.

"Is Annie *definitely* leaving us to live in Bo's house?" Again, she tilted the ball this way and that.

An answer floated up.

"Try again," it said.

Emma puffed out her breath. "Okay!" she said out loud, kind of annoyed. "*Is Annie moving away?*"

She tilted the globe round and round. "Try again," it said. *Again.*

Emma shook the globe so hard she almost dropped it, but she managed to grab it right before it hit the floor. Marmaduke came over to see what was going on. "Is Annie going to move?" Emma asked, not quite so loudly this time.

"Probably not," it answered.

Well! That was better.

She read through the booklet.

She heard little scuffling, whispering sounds in the hall. And then her door burst open and the twins bounced in, followed by Woof. The twins looked so cute in their little footie pajamas, giggling with one another.

"'Mergency, 'mergency! Nine one one!" Lizzie yelled, leaping onto the bed.

"Nine one one!" Ira yelled. "Nine one one!"

"'Mergency, 'mergency, nine one one!" they both sang together.

"What are you two talking about?" Emma said. She put down the ball and ran over to the bed and sat down. She reached for the twins and pulled them into her lap.

"At nursery school," Ira said. "That's what our teacher, Ms. Morris, told us. In an 'mergency, yell nine one one!"

"Yell nine one one?" Emma said, laughing. "I bet Ms. Morris said, '*call* nine one one,' right?"

Lizzie frowned. "Right," she said.

"Right," Ira said.

"Okay," Emma said. "Didn't she tell you to call on the phone? Not just to yell it?"

Lizzie looked at Ira and shrugged.

They both began to giggle. Ira stuck one finger in Emma's ear. And then they chanted all over again. "'Mergency, 'mergency, nine one one."

"Hush!" Emma said, turning away from Ira's finger. "You're hurting my head. Now what are you two doing up so early?"

"Daddy's making pancakes," Ira said.

"We're helping," Lizzie said. "But he couldn't find his slippers. He said it's a 'mergency, and he couldn't go down to the kitchen till he found them. We're helping look."

"Good luck," Emma said, and she let them go. They tumbled out of her arms and off the bed. They ran out of her room. Woof followed them.

So did Marmaduke.

"No!" Emma yelled, reaching for Marmaduke and almost falling off the bed. "Get back here."

But Marmaduke didn't come back. He was as fast as the twins, as fast as Woof, faster than all of them.

And Emma would probably have to spend the rest of the day looking for him.

Chapter Ten
Boring Family Meeting

Oh, no! Family meeting! That's what Daddy had announced at breakfast. There would be a family meeting right after breakfast. And Marmaduke was still missing, and Emma had no idea where he was hiding. She was certain he hadn't gotten out of the house, because Mom and Daddy both said that the doors hadn't been opened this morning, except once to let Woof out, and that was early, early, early, long before Emma woke up and cuddled with Marmaduke. So Marmaduke was around somewhere.

Emma despised, detested, and terribly hated family meetings. The meetings were supposed to be so the kids could talk about what was on their minds, and the grown-ups would listen. Like if the kids felt they needed more TV time or a later bedtime because they were growing up, Mom and Daddy listened. Then they thought about it and decided to agree. Or not agree. That's why Emma hated these meetings. Parents never agreed. Except once in a while for tiny stuff—like last week, they agreed that the kids could have two packages of gum a week instead of one. And Emma didn't even like gum.

That morning, they all met in the family playroom—Annie was there too. But this wasn't the usual meeting. This was all about Annie's wedding.

It began with Mom wanting everybody to learn the names of Annie's sisters. Because, Mom said, it wouldn't be nice to call them just "Hey," or "Hey you."

Annie just laughed. "Sure and you can learn them," she said, "but you won't be able to tell them apart anyway, except maybe for Nora, because she's taller than the others. Though not by much."

"Do they all look exactly alike?" Emma asked, thinking about the picture she had stolen. And feeling a little worried about it. Why hadn't she just asked Annie to give it to her? She didn't know. But she didn't know much about why she felt the way she felt about anything anymore.

"Well, once you get to know them, you'll be able to tell them apart," Annie said. "There are little differences. But at first, they really do all look alike. When we were little, folks often mistook us for twins or triplets or something."

"Are you all twins?" Ira asked.

"No, we're not twins," Annie said. "We just look alike."

"They're all pretty," Emma said. And then she felt shy, but it was true. Annie was very, very pretty, and so were the rest of the sisters.

Ira was frowning. Lizzie too.

"Then how can I tell which is you?" Lizzie asked.

"Because Annie will be the one in the long white dress," McClain said.

"Really?" Ira said.

"Really," Annie said. Emma giggled because she knew Annie wouldn't be wearing her wedding dress the whole time. "Okay," said Annie. "Here are their names. First, there's Nora. She's the eldest."

"And the tallest," Emma said.

"Right," Annie said.

"Then there's Bridget."

"She's the one who can bake a banana cake," Emma said.

Annie nodded and smiled.

"And then there're the twins, Meagan and Margaret."

"Twins? Like us?" Lizzie said.

"Almost like you," Annie said. "But they're both girls."

"How come?" Ira asked, frowning.

61

"Because," Annie said, "there are girl twins. And boy twins. And sometimes one of each, a boy and a girl, like you and Lizzie."

"There are?" Ira asked.

Annie nodded.

Ira shrugged. Lizzie also shrugged. Then they looked at one another. Lizzie began to giggle. Ira began to giggle. Emma had no idea what was so funny. But she knew the twins knew.

Suddenly, Emma wished that she had a twin. That way, one twin could want the wedding. And the other one could *not* want the wedding. And Emma wouldn't feel all mixed up inside.

"Do you have pictures of your sisters?" Daddy asked. "We could study them and put names and faces together that way."

"I could enlarge them on the computer," Tim said. "And you could put their names under them."

"Good idea!" Daddy said.

"I'll do it right this very minute," Annie said. "I have a picture in my room that shows them all together. It's the newest one. It came just this week. It's a *real* one, too, not just an electronic one, so it's much clearer." She got up and ran out of the room, Woof following her, the twins jumping up to trail behind too.

"Annie!" Emma called. "It's in my room."

Annie stopped and turned around. "It is?" she said.

Emma nodded.

"On my night table."

"Oh," Annie said. "Okay. Thanks."

Annie didn't ask why it was there, or how it had come to be there. She didn't ask anything.

Annie understood. She just did.

Chapter Eleven
Marmaduke Escapes

It was quiet in the family room. The only sound Emma could hear was the pitter-patter of Annie running up the stairs, her footsteps as light as a fairy. And the twins, tumbling after her, like puppies.

Daddy looked around. "Anyone have a question? A problem? Anything to talk over while we wait for Annie?"

McClain raised her hand. They had been taught to do that in family meetings because otherwise, everyone talked at once.

"Can I get a trampoline?" McClain asked. She had been asking that for two whole years. At least.

"I don't think so, McClain," Daddy said.

"No!" Mom said.

"Why not?" McClain asked.

"Because how many times have I told you? We

don't want you to break your neck," Mom said.

"*Especially* not right before the wedding," Emma said.

"Then can I get it after the wedding? Can I, Daddy? Mom?"

"No," Mom said.

"No," Daddy said.

McClain stuck out her lip.

"What else?" Mom asked. "Tim? You're quiet this morning."

Emma didn't know why Mom bothered to say that. Tim was *always* quiet. But Tim *was* more quiet than usual, and Emma wondered if Tim would say it: We're worried about Annie moving away. We're scared because everything's going to change. We're upset because Annie's taking away our safe place up on the third floor. And if they stay, Bo might not want us up there. Emma hoped Tim would say it. Then she wouldn't have to.

But he didn't. He only shook his head.

Coward! Emma thought. But she didn't say it, either. After a minute, Emma raised her hand.

"Yes, Emma?" Daddy asked.

"My room. I want it to be painted," Emma said. "I don't mind doing the work, but I need a little help—like moving the furniture. And Daddy, you said you'd get the paint and brushes."

"I already did it," Daddy said, smiling. "Early this morning, I went to Martin's paint store. With Woof. Before you were even awake. Everything's in the back laundry room, ready to go."

"You did? Oh, boy!" Emma said. "Thank you, Daddy, thank you. You bought the bright blue, right?"

"Yes," Daddy said. "But we're not going to paint your room yet, Emma. Not until after the wedding."

Emma screwed up her face. "But you said I could! You said so. You promised. Just last week, you said so."

"Emma," Mom said, using that calming voice that didn't calm anything inside Emma. "A week ago, we didn't know that we were going to have a wedding. We didn't know that we'd have to get flowers and food and music and rent tables and chairs and send out invitations and do all of that. And we only have two weeks to do it! And then the week after the wedding, it's Christmas! There is just too much to do."

"I told you I'd paint my room myself," Emma said. "I don't need help."

Daddy shook his head. "Emma," he said. "As soon as the wedding is over, we'll begin painting. I'll help. Fair enough?"

"No!" Emma said. "Not fair enough. Not fair at all. It's not like we're painting Annie's room!"

Mom and Daddy exchanged looks. Emma knew what that meant—they had something they wanted to say to one another, and they didn't want to say it in front of the kids.

Emma folded her arms and leaned back in her chair. Annie was messing things up.

"Besides, Emma," Daddy said, trying that *reasonable* voice like Mom's, "you need to clean up your room before you even begin to think about paint."

"My room's clean," Emma said.

Daddy laughed. "Depends what you mean by clean. I went to put away some of your laundry yesterday, and I couldn't get anything in your closet. It seemed ready to explode."

Emma shrugged. "Oh. Well. That."

Mom turned to Daddy. "I wonder what's taking Annie so long," she said. "Shall I go check?"

"Maybe she's cleaning *her* closet," Emma muttered.

"No, don't move!" Daddy said to Mom. "You sit. I'll go."

Mom sat back down. Mom was always popping up and around. Except when she hadn't had her coffee yet. But now, she had her coffee mug in one hand and she'd been drinking from it ever since their meeting had started.

"Mom?" Emma said, after Daddy had left. "Are you all right?"

"I'm fine, honey," Mom said. "Why do you ask?"

Emma shrugged.

"Are you worried about me?" Mom asked. "Or about Annie?"

"About *you*," Emma said. It was easier to say that. Besides, it was sort of true.

"What about me?" Mom asked. "Do I look like something's wrong? I'm having a baby, that's all. That's not an illness. It just makes me tired sometimes."

Again, Emma shrugged.

"What's wrong?" Mom asked. "Really, this isn't at all like you. Come here, come to me, sweetie." Mom put her coffee mug down and held out both arms.

Emma ran to Mom and settled in her lap. She didn't often settle in Mom's lap, and she didn't know why. More often, she ended up in Daddy's lap. Or Annie's. But Mom's lap did feel good.

"Daddy didn't mean to fuss at you about your closet," Mom said. "It's just that we have to keep the house tidy, especially with guests coming."

Emma nodded. She pressed against Mom. She couldn't ask the question. *What will we do without Annie here?*

Out of the corner of her eye, Emma could see Tim watching her. Well, why didn't *he* ask? He was the one who was so worried. At least, he was the one who worried the most.

In just a few minutes, Annie was back, Ira in her arms, and Daddy trailing behind, holding Lizzie's hand.

"I found it!" Annie said, smiling at Emma.

Emma nodded, then turned and buried her head in Mom's chest. She felt shy. And stupid. Why hadn't she asked Annie for the photo? And Annie didn't even wonder why Emma had taken it. Or at least she didn't say anything.

"Oh, wait!" Annie said. "I hear Bo's car. He can join our planning session. Is that all right with everybody?"

"Of course!" Mom said.

"Certainly," Daddy said. "It's also his wedding."

Emma had heard Bo's car too. She was accustomed to the sound of it, the way it rattled and hummed like a giant insect. She kept her head buried against Mom. In a few minutes, she heard Bo at the door and Woof barking a welcome.

And then there was a big ruckus, and everybody

began yelling and scrambling to their feet, even the twins.

"Come here, come back!" Bo yelled.

"Stop, stop you little rat!" McClain yelled.

"I'll get him," Tim shouted.

"No, no!" Annie was yelling.

Emma jumped out of Mom's lap. She raced into the hall just in time to see Marmaduke charge between Annie's legs, out the front door, and down the steps. He disappeared into the December morning, leaving only tiny footprints across the frozen grass.

Chapter Twelve

And Gets Rescued

Craziness. Crazy, mad ferret race.

Across the lawn. Around the back of the house. Into and out of the garage. Behind the fence where the trash pails were hidden.

Out front by the decorated Christmas tree.

Around back again.

The entire family was chasing Marmaduke, even the twins, still in their little footie pajamas.

Emma's heart was racing. She ran faster than anyone, and still, she couldn't get him. Once, she got her hands on him, but he squirted away from her, slipping under some bushes, where he peered out from under the branches.

"Okay, okay," Emma said softly. "It's okay. I'm not chasing you anymore. You can come out now."

She held out both hands, slowly, calmly.

He didn't move. He just crouched and watched

her, his wide black eyes like giant gumdrops.

And then Woof came galloping up. Emma threw herself at him, grabbing his collar. If he started chasing Marmaduke, they could end up miles away.

"Somebody!" Emma yelled. "Somebody come get Woof."

Tim appeared at Emma's side. "I've got him," he said calmly, taking hold of Woof's collar. "Is Marmaduke under there?"

Emma nodded. "I've got to get him calmed down, that's all. Then he'll come out. He just gets crazy."

"Imagine being Marmaduke's size," Tim said. "And all these monster-sized people after you."

Emma shook her head. "Take Woof into the house, okay?" she said. "And tell Mom and Daddy and everybody that I think I have Marmaduke, and nobody come out here and scare him away again. Okay?"

"Okay," Tim said. "Good. Now, come on, Woof. Let's go inside and get a dog cookie."

When they had gone, Emma looked at Marmaduke. "Come on, buddy," she coaxed. "Come back out. It's cold. I'm cold. You must be freezing."

As if he understood, he suddenly shuddered, shaking himself so that little drops of moisture flew off him. But he still didn't move toward Emma. In fact, he backed up a little.

"Marmaduke," Emma said quietly. "Will you please come out? I have a present for you."

Marmaduke crept forward a little. His big eyes got bigger and seemed blacker than ever. He tilted his head. He was asking what his present was.

"Ferret treats. I have a whole new box for you. I was saving it for your Christmas stocking, but I'll give you some now. If you come out."

Marmaduke frowned.

"Well, what else do you want?" Emma said. "Raisins? I know you love raisins, but they'll kill you. Remember that time you got into some? In the cookies? And how sick you got?"

Marmaduke crept forward a little.

He was close enough for Emma to get her hands on him. But he was quicker than she was. He had to be very close. *Very*. So she could grab him. And *hold on*. And right now, he was very wet and slippery looking.

"Come on, Marmaduke," Emma said. She was completely irritated with him. Her knees were freezing and her jeans were wet from kneeling on the cold ground.

Marmaduke didn't budge.

"Okay," Emma said. "Stay there. You'll just freeze to death. See if I care."

"Oh, but you don't mean that, do you?"

It was Bo. He had come up behind them so quietly that Emma hadn't heard a thing.

She turned to him and sighed. "I don't know. Right now, I feel that way. I mean, I halfway feel like that."

Bo smiled. "I know the feeling," he said. Then he added, "I have an idea. How about I go behind the bush. And you try to get your hands on him. That way, if he scoots back, I can catch him."

Emma took a deep breath. "Okay," she said. "But remember, he's slippery. Okay?"

"Okay," Bo said.

Emma waited while Bo circled the bush.

Then she reached for Marmaduke.

She got her hands on him, and he let her. He didn't try at all to escape. When she had him in her arms, he rested against her as if they were best friends. As if he hadn't tried to make a run for it. As if he hadn't made Emma chase him down and hadn't scared her half to death. As if he hadn't made Emma so mad that she hadn't cared if he came home. Not ever.

And she wondered what was wrong with her, to feel that way.

Chapter Thirteen

Family and Pets Go Beserk

In the days that followed, everyone in the house, pets too, became insane. It started with Woof. Delivery people came to the house with presents and extra tables and chairs for all the guests and food and flowers. And with each delivery, Woof barked and growled like a crazy dog. That wasn't like him. He was usually sweet to everyone. Emma used to think that if a burglar ever tried to get into the house, Woof would welcome him with big sloppy kisses. But not now.

Woof snarled at everyone. Emma wondered if maybe he was also worried that things would change when Annie got married. One UPS delivery person ran back to his truck and hid until Bo discovered him shivering with fear. Bo held Woof back long enough for the man to get his delivery done. And when the man had finished, he yelled, "Never again! I've made deliveries to the lunatic hospitals, but this place is much worse."

When Woof wasn't trying to terrorize the delivery people, he acted like a mad dog, running round and round and round and round, chasing his tail, which he didn't have much of because he was a poodle. He bumped into furniture and knocked things off tables. One night, Daddy grabbed him by the collar, sat him down, and looked right into his eyes. "You," Daddy said, "are going straight to the cellar if you don't settle down. Understand?"

Woof nodded.

"You sure?" Daddy said.

Again, Woof nodded.

But Woof didn't settle down. And Daddy didn't send him to the cellar either.

Then Kelley escaped and ran under the back steps and didn't come out for two whole days. McClain lay on her tummy most of one freezing cold day, trying to coax her out. When Kelley finally emerged, she was all squashed looking. Her usually fluffy fur was flat and dirty and still kind of blue in spots from the paint, and McClain gave her a bath. McClain made a terrible mess in the bathroom. Then McClain refused to clean it up. "Later," she said, which Emma knew meant never. McClain said Kelley had been *traumatized* and needed to be held for a while. And how did McClain even know that word?

Emma decided the animals had gone nuts. First Marmaduke. Then Kelley. Then Woof. You'd think they were the ones getting married.

Mom and Daddy and Annie and Bo were all extra busy with wedding plans and none of them seemed to have time for Emma—or anybody else, for that matter. Mom and Daddy had even stopped reading to the kids before bedtime. Mom said if she sat down by a bed, she'd fall asleep and not get up till morning. Both she and Daddy had taken a week off work to plan the wedding and make sure everything went smoothly.

Mom was always at the desk in the family room, writing things on little sticky notes and putting them here and there on her desk and all over the computer. It looked a mess, sort of like Emma's desk.

Some days, Mom seemed totally exasperated with the people on the phone, even though Emma could tell that Mom tried to sound calm. Emma even thought Mom once mouthed the word "stupid," but she couldn't be sure. And some days, Mom was exasperated with the kids, too, even when they hadn't done anything wrong.

Emma wouldn't have minded the madhouse so

much. She liked it when things were crazy. People, even moms, were allowed to get upset sometimes. But they weren't allowed to get mad at the kids when the kids hadn't done anything wrong. Like one day, Emma had mentioned that she really wished she could paint her room. Mom threw her pencil down on her desk and stalked out of the room, as if she were on fire.

"I didn't even *ask!*" Emma said to the empty room. "I just said I'd like to."

Then the twins, who were always sweet as candy buttons to each other, turned into little demons. One morning, while Ira was sitting and coloring at the small work table, Lizzie walked over and picked up his free hand from the table. She put it in her mouth. And bit it. They hadn't had a fight. They hadn't been making faces at each other. It was as if Lizzie suddenly decided it might be a good idea. Ira didn't think it was such a good idea. He screamed. Tiny red teeth marks appeared on the back of his hand. When he howled, Lizzie looked surprised and started howling too. Then Mom did something Emma had never seen her do before. She jumped up from her desk, picked Lizzie up and smacked her little bottom. Quite hard. Then Daddy began fussing, not over Lizzie, not over Ira, but over Mom! It was as if Mom was the one who'd been biting. Or bitten.

That's when Emma decided that they had all lost their minds. Finally, the day came when Mom and Daddy said they thought the plans were all in place. Annie would come down the front stairs in her wedding gown—her mother was making the gown—and step into the long wide hallway, the one where the new flooring had just been installed. Then, she'd walk to the back of the hall toward the playroom/family room. The doors would be wide open—they were double doors, sort of like church doors, that were almost always kept closed to keep toys and pets and kids inside—and the room would be decked out in pink poinsettias. Mom had bought tons of them. Some were on the mantle; bunches of them were stacked on either side of the fireplace; and there were more along the long, low windowsills. The minister would be waiting by the fireplace, where she would perform the wedding ceremony. (Daddy said it seemed funny to have a woman minister, and Mom glared at him when he said that. Daddy quickly said, "Didn't mean anything, didn't mean anything," and he didn't say it again.)

Daddy had hired a violinist who would walk around playing music. (Ira had wanted drums, but Daddy said no.) After the wedding ceremony, there would be a dinner served in the dining room and also the living room, where extra seats and tables would be set up for all the guests. Bo had two brothers and two sisters, and they were bringing their girlfriends and boyfriends, and then there were Bo's mom and dad and grandparents. There would be a ton of people.

Mom had picked out the sweetest little suit for Ira—short pants but with a jacket, so he looked like a little man. He was going to carry the wedding ring on a tiny pillow and give it to Bo when the minister asked for it. Mom had it pinned to the pillow so it wouldn't roll off and disappear.

She had also chosen two pale blue dresses, a short, fluffy one for Lizzie and a short one in a different style for McClain. Mom worried because McClain had scrapes and bruises and scratches up and down her legs from tumbling and jumping around. So Mom bought white tights to cover her bruised legs. McClain fell in love with her dress and wanted to wear it immediately. And she had a major tantrum fit when Mom said no, period, absolutely not.

Emma's dress was the best, though. She had gone with Annie to pick it out, but not with Mom. That was good because Emma knew that Mom would choose a baby-type dress. Emma's dress was pink, pale pink. Annie said that as a junior bridesmaid, she should look different, special. It had something called a sweetheart neck that dipped a little in the front, but not too much. And it was long, all the way to the floor. There were velvet bows at the waist and a long sash that tied around her middle. Emma thought it was the most beautiful dress ever.

The biggest plan, though, even bigger than Emma getting her own dress for the wedding, was that the sisters and their mum were arriving in just two days. Daddy had gone ahead and hired a limousine to pick them up, but it was going to be a surprise. Emma worried that the girls wouldn't know the limo was meant for them. But Daddy said the limo driver would be holding up a sign with their names printed on it.

Mom had prepared the guest room and put clean linens on the beds. Emma had helped by putting flowers in a vase on the nightstand. Some of the sisters, and probably their mom too, would sleep there, and the other sisters would sleep up in Annie's apartment.

Emma wondered if they would have a fight over who slept where. If she were one of the sisters, she would want to sleep near Annie.

Finally everything was ready. And there was nothing left to do for two whole days.

Nothing to do but wait and wonder.

That night, Emma had a shower and opened her notebook. She wrote about how her family had become nuts, and how she was worried about what would happen after the wedding, especially with new baby coming, and could they manage without Annie, even for the few days she'd be taking off for her honeymoon.

And then it started to rain.

It rained. And rained. And rained. It wasn't a gentle rain, the kind that fell in the spring and summer. This was December, and it was an icy rain, making little snicking sounds against the windowpanes. Every now and then, there was even the sound of thunder rumbling.

Daddy said it was a good thing the sisters weren't coming until tomorrow, because the storm would delay all flights.

Annie helped Mom and Daddy get everyone bathed and tucked into bed with the lights out. Then, maybe because everyone was tired out from all the excitement, the twins and McClain settled down pretty fast.

Tim went to bed, saying he wanted to sit up and read a while.

Emma went to her room and climbed in bed. But she didn't sleep and she didn't read. She lay awake. Thinking. Plotting.

While the thunder still rumbled—and, for heaven's sake, it was the middle of winter!—Emma worried about Tim.

She worried about having no safe place for either of them to go.

And so, in the middle of the night, with the storm still raging and blowing, Emma made a decision.

She sat up in bed, smiling to herself. A perfect plan was already forming in her head.

Chapter Fourteen
Emma's Best Plan Ever

Wide awake now, Emma thought about a book she'd read recently. It was about a girl on a prairie. When there was a storm, the girl and her family would go down into a storm cellar to keep from getting blown away or bonked on the head by a flying object.

Emma thought if she painted her closet, she'd have a perfect place for herself. It could be her storm closet, her own place to go to if Annie did that stinky, mean thing and moved away.

The storm continued to rage outside. It was very late, after twelve according to Emma's Mickey Mouse watch.

Before Emma started painting, she had to be sure her bedroom door was closed tight. If Mom or Daddy heard her up in the middle of the night, they'd be really angry.

Emma walked across the room and pushed against her bedroom door. Something pushed back on the other side.

She opened the door a crack. Woof. He always lay just outside her door.

She opened the door wider to let him in. "Hey Woof," she whispered. "You can come help, but don't make any noise. And don't get into anything. Okay?"

He nodded.

Emma closed the door and went over to her closet. It was enormous and ran way back, with a ceiling that slanted downward. Emma had always loved hiding here, even when she was a little kid.

Now—well, Daddy was right about the mess. The closet was so jammed full of stuff, she didn't know where to begin. She just stood there, staring at it. Soccer stuff. Clothes. Winter coats. Summer flip-flops. Boots. Ice skates. Where did all that come from? She didn't remember even having ice skates.

Emma tried tidying things up, shoving things aside, and putting stuff on shelves. There weren't enough shelves to hold anything.

She'd have to re-organize. That was something she wasn't very good at.

Sports equipment first. She could put it in a big pile, and shove it all to one side. Then she could add all the other stuff. After that, she'd be able to figure out what to get rid of, what didn't fit her anymore, and what to keep. She discovered six, no seven, no *eight* pairs of soccer cleats! She stared down at one of the shoes in her hand. It was so tiny; she couldn't believe her feet had once been that small!

No. Impossible. She looked at her watch. It was almost one o'clock. Forget about organizing. She'd just empty the closet and worry about organizing everything later.

Soon, she had pulled everything out of her whole closet. But now her room was a mess! There was an enormous pile of stuff that stretched all the way to the window seat. Then Emma had an idea. She'd put a big blanket over the mess to hide it.

She went out in the hall to the linen closet. She pulled out a huge gray quilt that the family sometimes used when they went camping. She brought it back to her room. She closed her door tightly and then threw the blanket over the huge pile of stuff. Good. It looked like an elephant, a huge gray elephant, lying in her room. Emma even fiddled around with a softball bat under the blanket to make it look like a trunk.

Emma was afraid for a moment that maybe what she was doing was not right. But it wasn't really wrong, either. Mom and Daddy had said no to her painting her room. They hadn't said anything at all about not painting her closet. Besides, Daddy had said the closet needed tidying.

With nothing in it now, it was really tidy.

Emma tiptoed down the stairs. The whole house was dark, no light peeping out from under anyone's door. Emma loved her room and her house, but in the dark in the middle of the night, it felt a little creepy. She could have gone back to her room to get Woof to accompany her, but he tended to make noise. She'd be all right.

She went to the back laundry room where Daddy had stored the paint. There, she found the paint and brushes, and then the paint opener thing. She brought it all back upstairs to her room.

Emma went to the closet and worked at opening one of the paint cans. The opener was hard to use. Emma stuck it under the lid and then pried it upward. The lid loosened, and Emma lifted it off. She smiled down at the paint in the can. Blue! A bright electric blue. A wonderful electric blue. What first? Well, dip the paintbrush in the paint, and wipe it along the side of the can, the way she'd learned when she'd helped Daddy paint the twins' bedroom. Then up and down, across the wall. Up and down. Woof kept dancing around by the closet

87

door and Emma kept pushing him back. She didn't want his fur to turn all blue, like Kelley's had done.

But he kept pushing his way in, so eventually, Emma said all right. "But just don't lean against the wall, okay?"

Woof nodded.

"I mean it," Emma said.

Again, Woof nodded. He stayed very still in the center of the closet.

It didn't take long before Emma had an entire wall finished. Then she started on the second wall. And then the back wall. Although the closet was big, the painting went pretty fast. When Emma was almost finished, she did a little decorating, making some swirls with the paint across the back. It looked kind of like a sky. The only hard part was wiping up the spills. That got kind of messy.

Although Emma had been careful not to load the brush up with too much paint, she still made drips. After the first wall, however, she kind of caught on. Emma looked around for something to use to wipe up the spills.

She found what she needed in the elephant pile—an old soccer shirt from when her team was called The Hornets and they wore yellow shirts. It would do for now. She'd throw it in the wash tomorrow.

She wiped up the drips with the shirt. The floor got kind of streaky blue. Emma frowned at it. The bottoms of her feet were kind of blue, too, and wherever she stepped, there were blue footprints. It was actually kind of cute. There were also dog prints. Emma thought that maybe when Mom and Daddy finally agreed her room could be painted, Daddy would let her make footprints across the floor. Anyway, it was washable paint. At least that's what the labels on the cans said.

Carefully, Emma set the paintbrush down on top of one of the lids. She stepped back and looked at the painted walls. Beautiful. She was tired though, and holding the paintbrush had made a blister on her hand. But she was finished.

"So?" Emma said, looking down at Woof and backing out of the closet. "What do you think?"

Colorful, Woof answered. *Wonderful*. But of course, he didn't say that out loud.

"I think so too," Emma said.

Woof took a tentative step into the closet. He looked back at Emma, as if to ask if that was all right.

"It's okay. Just don't touch the walls," she said.

Woof nodded. He stepped into the closet very daintily. He was really good at walking that way. Most poodles were, Daddy had told Emma once.

In dog shows, they were even rated on how prettily they could walk.

"You're very handsome," Emma told him. Woof tilted his head. Emma knew he liked it when she said nice things about him.

He turned around and went further into the closet. And stepped right on the paint can lid. Bright blue paint spilled all over his dainty paws. The paws that made oh-so-dainty paw prints now, each time he took a dainty step.

Chapter Fifteen
Almost Found Out

When the thunder rolled in, it was so loud at first that Emma jumped. It sounded as if a truck had run right smack into the house or into her bedroom.

Emma sucked in her breath. Tim was sure to be up and out of bed, looking for her or Annie.

Emma opened her bedroom door and peeked out into the hall. Tim opened his door at the same time, and peeked into the hall too.

Emma motioned to him. "Come here. You can come to my room," she whispered.

"Okay," he said.

He ran the few steps down the hall, his flashlight bobbing around.

Flashlight? Honestly, how did he get a flashlight so quick? He probably had it right by his bed. Emma had a flashlight, too, but she had no idea where it was. And if she found it, she knew the batteries would be dead.

Emma held the door open for him. "Come on in. You can sleep in bed with me. Or I'll share my storm closet with you."

"What stinks in here?" Tim said, sniffing and looking around.

Emma smiled. "Paint. But it's not too stinky, is it?"

"Yes, it is," Tim said. "If you're painting in here, Mom and Daddy are going to kill you."

"I'm not painting my room," Emma said. "Just the inside of my closet. And they didn't say I couldn't paint my closet. Want to see? You can come in too. It's my storm closet."

"Why?" Tim asked.

"*Why?*" Emma said. "You know why. Annie? Right?"

"Oh," Tim said, and he nodded.

Emma held Woof back while they both looked into the closet.

"Wow! Cool," Tim said. Then he looked around. "Where'd you put all your stuff?"

Emma pointed to the elephant.

"Oh," Tim said.

"And I'm going to put pillows in here and quilts

and even a lamp so I can read, and lots of books. Maybe food too."

Tim just stood there, staring and shaking his head. "Very cool," he said eventually. "Think it will work?"

Emma knew what he meant. She didn't have to ask. She just nodded. "I'm sure it will."

"Can I bring my own pillows and stuff?"

Emma nodded. "Anything. Even your computer if you want."

"Be right back," Tim said. And he ran out the door and down the hall to his room. He returned in a minute, dragging his huge quilt and a bunch of pillows.

Thunder roared and rattled the house once more.

"The light just went on in Mom and Daddy's room," Tim said.

"Uh-oh," Emma said. "Let's just get into my bed. If they look in, we'll be sound asleep."

"I can't fall asleep that fast," Tim said.

Emma sighed. "Don't be dopey. Can't you pretend?"

"Daddy's going to smell the paint."

"I'll open a window," Emma said. "Oops. No, I can't. It's raining too hard."

There was another streak of lightning, and then

another enormous thunderclap. It actually shook the house.

Emma knew that Mom and Daddy would be up, checking that nobody was awake or scared. She hoped the twins would start crying. And then she had a thought: She and Tim could just go out in the hall themselves and close the bedroom door behind them. She'd say that the storm woke her up. Then she'd say she was fine, say good night, and go to the bathroom or something, and she and Tim could head back to her room. She didn't think Daddy would come in if he could see they were okay.

"Come on, Tim," she said. "Come with me."

"Where are we going?"

"Just come!" Emma said. "Hurry." To herself she said, *my life might depend on it.*

Tim made a face, but he followed Emma out of the room.

Sure enough, both Mom and Daddy were in the hall. They had just come out of the twins' room. Mom was wearing one of Daddy's old t-shirts. Emma thought she looked like a teenager. Daddy looked weird. His hair was all tousled and queer, as if he'd been standing on his head in his sleep.

"Where's Tim?" Mom said. "He's not in his room."

And then she saw him behind Emma. "You guys okay?" Mom said. "That was some terrific thunder. It scared the wits out of me."

Emma nodded. "Scared me too," she said. "We're not supposed to have thunderstorms in winter."

"Tim?" Daddy said. "You okay?"

"I'm okay," Tim said. "But it's winter. I thought thunderstorms would be gone by now."

"True," Daddy said. "But it happens. Okay, Tim, back to your room now. You, too, Emma."

"I told Tim he could stay in my room tonight," Emma said.

"Oh," Mom said. "Okay."

Daddy nodded. "Okay, Tim. That's fine."

Everybody knew that Tim was scared of thunder and lightning storms, strange cats, new teachers, and monsters in the closets. But nobody made a big deal out of any of it, so Tim wouldn't be embarrassed. Mom said he'd grow out of it eventually.

"All right, kiddos," Daddy said. "Bedtime." He turned to Mom. "Something smells strange," he said. "Do you smell it?"

Mom sniffed. She shook her head. "No. I don't smell anything," she said.

"Neither do I," Emma said.

"Me, neither," Tim said. "Good night."

"Good night," Mom said. And she went into their bedroom.

"Want me to tuck you guys in?" Daddy asked.

"No!" Emma and Tim both said together.

"Oh, okay," Daddy said. He frowned. Emma thought he looked sad. She wondered if maybe his feelings were hurt. When he turned toward his bedroom, she ran down the hall after him. "Wait, Daddy!" she said, and she threw her arms around him. "Night," she whispered. "I love you."

"Love you too, little rascal," Daddy said, and he hugged her.

Emma stood back and waited till Daddy had shut his and Mom's bedroom door, before she went back to her room.

"Whew!" she said, when she and Tim were safely inside with the door shut. "That was close. Do you think they suspected anything?"

"Daddy did," Tim said.

"I know," Emma said. "But then he didn't."

"I thought he seemed sad," Tim said. "When we said we didn't want tucking in."

"I know," Emma said. "That's why I gave him a hug. Okay, now bring your pillows and blankets into the closet. I'll get mine. And then help me bring in the night table. And the lamp."

Soon, they were settled in the storm closet with the door open. Emma had chosen one side, Tim the other. The night table and lamp were between them. And Woof. Emma examined his feet. They were quite blue but finally dry. She had brought Marmaduke in too, so he wouldn't feel left out, but she kept him in his cage. He was so nosey when he was in a new place. Emma didn't want him exploring all over the inside of the closet and keeping her awake. It was almost three in the morning! She hadn't slept a wink.

And then, after a few minutes, they all settled down and fell sleep, all four of them.

Emma, Tim, Woof, and Marmaduke too.

Chapter Sixteen
Marmaduke Is Very Sick

When Emma awoke in the morning, for a minute she didn't know where she was. Why was Tim on the floor beside her? Why was she on the floor? Sun was streaming in from somewhere. Where was she?

And then she remembered. She was in her storm closet. Wonderful. Colorful.

Woof was awake now, stretching and prancing around, wanting to be let out.

"Just a minute," Emma told him. She bent over Marmaduke's cage. "Marmaduke needs to be let out too."

"Hey, buddy!" she said, reaching in for Marmaduke. And then she screamed. "Mom! Daddy! Help!"

Marmaduke was lying on his back. His legs were straight up in the air. He looked—dead! Emma lifted him out. He didn't snuggle up to her. He just lay against her like he was a pretend animal, like one of McClain's stuffed animals.

Emma raced down the hall with him and banged open the door to Mom and Daddy's room, even though she was supposed to knock first.

"Mom! Daddy!" she cried. "Help. I think Marmaduke's . . . " She couldn't say the word. She was thinking "dead," but she said "sick."

Mom and Daddy were sitting up in bed. Mom already had her coffee mug in her hand. McClain was snuggled in between them, holding the TV remote. Some cartoon was roaring from the TV in the corner.

"What is it?" Mom asked, looking alarmed. "What's happened?"

"Something. I don't know. Marmaduke's sick. Call Dr. Pete. Can we take Marmaduke over to him right away?"

Daddy reached for Marmaduke. Emma didn't want to let him out of her arms, but maybe Daddy could do mouth-to-mouth breathing on him.

She held him out toward Daddy.

Marmaduke opened one eye.

"Oh, he's not dead. Oh, he's not!" Emma cried.

McClain frowned at him. "His gills aren't moving."

Daddy began stroking Marmaduke's head. "What's up, little buddy?" Daddy asked. "You got a tummy ache or something? You ate something that didn't agree with you?"

"Can we take him? Can we take him now?" Emma asked. "Can we take him to Dr. Pete *right now*, this second?"

Mom was already on the phone. Emma knew she was calling Dr. Pete. Mom talked for a minute, then hung up and turned to Emma. "Go get some clothes on," she said. "Dr. Pete's waiting for you. Daddy will take you."

Emma reached for Marmaduke.

"Why don't you just leave him here," Mom said. "He's comfortable now. Go on, get dressed. He'll be all right without you for a minute. I'll watch him."

Emma raced back down the hall to her room.

Tim was still sound asleep in the storm closet.

Emma threw on jeans, a sweatshirt, and her flip-flops and was back in Mom and Daddy's room in two seconds flat. She didn't even stop to go to the bathroom or to brush her teeth.

Daddy was in his and Mom's bathroom, the door closed. Emma began hopping back and forth from one foot to the other. "Hurry up, Daddy!" she called through the door. "Come on, hurry up!"

"I'm coming!" Daddy said.

Emma gently lifted Marmaduke off the bed. He opened both eyes and looked at Emma, then closed his eyes again. He seemed to be very tired.

Oh! That's all, Emma thought. *He's just tired. He was up half the night just like me and Tim.* But Marmaduke was often up half the night. Something was wrong. He'd never acted like this before.

Emma held him close to her chest, and when Daddy came out of the bathroom, she very carefully carried Marmaduke down the stairs and outdoors to the car.

Neither Emma nor Daddy said much as they drove the few blocks to Dr. Pete's office. Emma held Marmaduke next to her face, murmuring over and over again, "Please don't die, please don't die, please, please, please."

When they pulled up in front of the vet's office, Emma was out of the car and up the steps, almost before Daddy had parked.

She burst into the waiting room. No one was there—no dogs or cats or people. No nurse or receptionist either. She ran through the offices to the examining rooms where she had gone with Marmaduke and Woof and Kelley a gazillion times.

Dr. Pete was getting up from his desk when Emma burst in.

"Look!" Emma cried. "Look, he's sick, really, really sick."

Dr. Pete reached for Marmaduke and gently laid him on an examining table. Marmaduke didn't even try to squirm away.

"What's happened, old friend?" Dr. Pete said, bending over Marmaduke. "You don't look so hot."

"Is he dying?" Emma said.

"Well," Dr. Pete said, "probably not. He's a strong little guy. But let's take a look at him before I say anything for sure."

Dr. Pete put his stethoscope thing into his own ears and put one end against Marmaduke's little chest. Daddy had come in by then and was standing at the door. He crossed the room and stood beside Emma.

Dr. Pete was frowning.

"Is he okay?" Emma asked.

"Not exactly," Dr. Pete said. "But I don't know what's happened to him. Could he have ingested something poisonous?"

Emma didn't understand.

"*Eaten* something, *eaten* something poisonous?" Dr. Pete said.

"No!" Emma said. "What could he have eaten that's poisonous?"

102

Dr. Pete looked at Daddy. "You don't have rat poison or something like that around the house, do you?"

"No!" Daddy said. "We don't have rats, and we'd never put poison down with the kiddos around."

"Weed killer, something like that?" Dr. Pete went on. "Even something that he might have breathed in? His chest sounds noisy."

"What's that mean?" Emma asked.

"Well, he might have pneumonia. Something's gotten into his airways."

Emma looked at Daddy.

Daddy was shaking his head.

"No fumes, no laying tiles, nothing like that?" Dr. Pete asked.

Again, Daddy shook his head. "We put down flooring and new carpets, but that was weeks ago."

"No painting, not even outside?" Dr. Pete said.

Daddy shook his head.

Uh, oh. Paint. In the closet.

Dr. Pete was frowning harder now, his face screwed up.

"Um," Emma said. "I did paint. Just a little bit. In my closet."

"What?" Daddy said.

"Well, you said I had to clean up in there."

"Wait a minute," Dr. Pete said. "What kind of paint? And was Marmaduke in the closet when you painted?"

Emma shook her head. She felt totally terrified. Marmaduke was going to die and it was all her fault. And Daddy was going to kill her. "Afterward, he was," she answered. "After I was all finished. But I kept him in his cage. So he didn't eat any paint, I know that. I know it for sure."

"What kind of paint?" Dr. Pete said.

"Electric blue," Emma said.

Dr. Pete was looking at Daddy. "Is it oil based?"

Daddy frowned. "I don't remember. All I know is, I told the guy at the paint store that it had to be washable."

Dr. Pete went to one of his cabinets and took out some ugly looking things. Emma thought they were those mean needles that Marmaduke sometimes had to have. Emma called them shots, but Dr. Pete said they were immunizations—like for rabies. The other animals, Woof and Kelley, had had shots too. So had Emma and the kids, although not here and not for rabies.

Emma went over to the exam table. She picked up Marmaduke and held him to her. He opened his eyes. He struggled to get up on her shoulder and look around.

"Oh, you're better, aren't you? Don't worry about the shot, I'll hold you."

"Well," Dr. Pete said. "I think Marmaduke is feeling better already. I think perhaps he needed to breathe some fresh air."

"Oh, is that all?" Emma said. "I'm so happy. Can I take him home now?"

"I don't think so," Dr. Pete said. "I want to keep him here for a day or two and watch him. I need to be sure the fumes haven't harmed him in any way. His kidneys or liver."

"Would that be bad?" Emma asked.

"Let's not worry about it," Dr. Pete said. "He's looking better already, so I think he's going to be okay."

"Then why can't he come home with me?"

"Emma," Daddy said. "Don't be a pest. Dr. Pete knows best. Besides, you have other things to worry about."

Emma was quiet for a minute. And then she said, "I only painted the closet."

"*Oh?*" Daddy said. "*Only?*"

"Yes!" Emma replied. "You said don't paint my room. You didn't say anything about my closet, and you said I should tidy it up. Wait till you see it. It's beautiful. Woof thinks so too."

"Was Woof with you in the closet?" Dr. Pete asked.

"Yes," Emma said, and her heart started thumping hard again. "Is he going to get sick too?"

"I don't think so," Dr. Pete said. "Big animals don't react the way small ones do. But maybe you should bring him in for a look-see, just to make sure."

"Okay," Emma said. "I'll run home and get him right now. Okay, Daddy?"

Daddy nodded, and Emma raced out of the office and down the few blocks to home.

As she went, she said the same prayer she had whispered in the car, over and over again. But this time for Woof. "Please don't die, please don't die. Please, please, *please* don't die."

Chapter Seventeen
Woof Is Very Blue

Emma was wearing flip-flops and it was freezing out. Not only were her feet cold, but it was also hard to run in flip-flops.

"Mom?" she called, when she got in the house. "Mom! I need Woof."

"He's up here," Mom called down. "What's happening?"

Emma grabbed Woof's leash from the hook by the back door, raced up the stairs with the leash in her hand, and kicked off her flip-flops as she went. Mom was still curled up in bed with McClain.

"Dr. Pete wants to check him out. He thinks that maybe the paint poisoned Marmaduke, and he wants to check Woof too."

"Is Marmaduke okay?" McClain asked.

Emma nodded. "He's fine now," she said. She couldn't say anything else.

"What paint?" Mom said.

Emma shrugged. She bent and clipped Woof's leash to his collar. "Hold on. I'll be right back," she said.

She ran down the hall to her room. She found her socks and gym shoes and pulled them on. Then she went back to get Woof.

"Emma!" Mom said. "What is going on? What paint are you talking about?"

Emma shrugged. "Oh, you know," she said. "But I have to go now. Dr. Pete needs to check that Woof's okay. And he wants to do it right away."

Mom sighed. "I can't wait to hear," she said.

Emma could tell that Mom was mad. But it didn't matter to Emma, not right that minute. All that mattered was that Marmaduke and Woof were all right. Emma ran down the steps, and Woof galloped along beside her. He seemed his usual self, not droopy or fainting like Marmaduke had been.

Together, they ran the few blocks to Dr. Pete's office. It was much easier this time, now that Emma had on regular shoes.

They burst in and found Daddy sitting and holding Marmaduke in his arms. Dr. Pete was sitting in his desk chair, the two of them talking.

Dr. Pete stood up when Emma and Woof came in.

Woof began leaping around, sniffing at everything, the way he always did in Dr. Pete's office. Unlike some dogs Emma had seen there, Woof didn't mind at all going to the vet. He liked Dr. Pete.

"Well," Dr. Pete said, smiling. "Woof doesn't seem like a sick dog to me."

"Oh, I'm so happy!" Emma said. "But what about Marmaduke? Is Marmaduke okay?" She looked over at Daddy. Marmaduke seemed limp in Daddy's arms, like maybe he was . . .

But she couldn't say the word, not even in her head. "He looks . . . queer," was all she could say. "Are you sure he's okay?"

"I've given him an antihistamine," Dr. Pete said. "That will make him sleepy for a while. But I think he'll be all right."

"But you're not sure?" Emma asked.

"Pretty sure," Dr. Pete said. And then he crouched down in front of Woof. "And how are you, my good man?" he asked.

Woof gave Dr. Pete a big sloppy kiss. Dr. Pete laughed. He didn't even wipe off the kiss. Instead, he put his stethoscope to Woof's chest and listened for a minute. He moved it here and there on Woof. Woof was used to this. He stood as still as a statue, as if he knew that's what he was supposed to do.

After a minute, Dr. Pete tucked the stethoscope into his jacket pocket and patted Woof, ruffling his head and ears. He lifted Woof's front paw and examined it, first one paw, then the other. He frowned.

"What's this?" he said.

Emma shrugged. "Just the paint," she said. "Like I told you about. Just a little."

"I think we should wash it off," Dr. Pete said. "It could hurt him."

"Hurt him how?" Emma asked, her heart thumping hard again.

"It will stiffen," Dr. Pete said. "And he'll start gnawing at it. Let me get something to wash him with."

Dr. Pete went to one of his cabinets and came back with a bottle and a rag. He lifted Woof's front paw and rubbed it.

Woof began licking it.

"Stop it, you old dog, you," Dr. Pete said, shoving Woof's head away.

"He's not old," Emma said. "He's just five. We got him when McClain was born."

"Well, hold onto him," Dr. Pete said. "Hold his head while I go to work on his paws. We don't want him to lick any of that paint off."

"Why not?" Emma asked.

Dr. Pete didn't answer. He just went about

cleaning Woof's paws for quite a while. Only Woof wasn't patient. He wanted to get going and Emma had a hard time holding him still. He kept trying to move this way and that.

Dr. Pete's phone began ringing. It rang and rang. Emma looked at it wildly. It might be Mom. Trying to see what was going on. Emma didn't want Mom to know, not right now. She didn't want anyone to know. She felt so guilty.

Finally, Emma asked, "Aren't you going to answer your phone?"

"The service will pick up," Dr. Pete answered. Then he added, "There's quite a lot of paint on his paws. I can't imagine what your floors look like."

"Oh, they're okay," Emma said. She was glad her back was to Daddy.

"They better be, Emma," Daddy said. "If you've ruined that new hall floor you'll be in more trouble than you've ever been in your life."

"Woof didn't even go downstairs," Emma said.

"Really?" Daddy said. "Then how did he get outside?"

He jumped out the window. He flew. But Emma didn't say those things out loud. She figured she was already in enough trouble.

"He just stayed in my room," she said. But she wasn't sure that was exactly true. When she had awakened, when she saw how Marmaduke looked—as if he were . . . that D word that she couldn't say—she had raced to Mom and Daddy's room. She hadn't paid attention at all to where Woof went roaming. And maybe he had stepped into the open paint can again. Emma knew she hadn't closed it up. She'd tried but the lid had got stuck so she'd just left the can open on the floor by her bed.

"Okay," Dr. Pete said finally. "I think I have the worst of it off. But if he starts gnawing at his feet, I want you to bring him back here. Okay? Then we'll have to use something stronger on him. The pads on poodles' feet are tender, so I want to go slowly."

Emma stood up. She let go of Woof's head and right away, he started snooping around, the way he always did.

"Do I have to leave Marmaduke here?" Emma asked.

Dr. Pete nodded. "You do," he said.

"And you'll take good care of him?"

"Of course," Dr. Pete said.

"But what if he gets . . . like, worse? Will you call me?"

"He won't get worse," Dr. Pete said.

"You sure?"

"Pretty sure."

"Emma," Daddy said. "Let's go home. I think it's time we had a talk. And time to see what the floors look like."

"Oh, okay," Emma said.

And then she thought, *I really don't want to drive home with Daddy.* If he wanted to talk, Emma was pretty sure she knew what he was going to say.

"I'll walk home with Woof," she added.

She grabbed his leash, hooked it onto his collar, and darted out of the office. Before Daddy could say a word.

Chapter Eighteen

Emma's Big, Big, Big Trouble

Emma took the long way home, the long, long slow way home. She let Woof sniff at every spot he wanted to sniff at, and she let him pee on all his favorite trees and bushes. Then she walked around the block again. She did this till she couldn't put off going home any longer.

When she walked up the driveway, she noticed Annie's car wasn't there. If Annie were home, she would help Emma so that Mom and Daddy wouldn't be so mad. But then Emma remembered that this was the day Annie had arranged to do "girl" things with her friends. They were getting manicures and pedicures and Annie planned to have her hair done. Annie had beautiful long red hair, and sometimes, she liked to wear it twisted up on top of her head. Emma liked it better when it lay around her shoulders.

Oh, well, there was nothing she could do to bring Annie home. Emma would have to face Mom and Daddy on her own.

Emma went in the back door, hung Woof's leash on the hook, and called, "I'm home!"

"We're in here," Mom called from the family room.

McClain came bursting out of the family room. "What took you so long?" she said. "Daddy's been home for ages. Where's Marmaduke?"

"At Dr. Pete's," Emma said.

"Is he dead?" McClain said.

"No!" Emma said. "Don't say that word. Now, where's everybody?"

"In there," McClain said, nodding her head toward the family room.

"Are they really mad?" Emma asked.

McClain nodded. "Yup."

"What did they say?"

McClain shrugged. "Something . . . I don't know. Just about Annie and the wedding. And how you made a big mess. Daddy's trying to find a floor fisher person."

"Floor fisher?" Emma asked.

McClain nodded.

"What's that?" Emma said.

McClain shrugged.

"Okay," Emma said. "Here goes." And she went to join the family in the big room.

When she opened the door, she saw the usual: On the floor by the windows, the twins were playing with a toy. It looked like a small parking car garage. They didn't even look up to say hi.

Tim was sprawled in the big fluffy chair, reading. He sort of waved at Emma. McClain plopped down on the rug, pulling Kelley into her arms. She had a string in her hand and tried to tease Kelly into leaping after it. Kelley looked bored.

Mom was sitting at one end of the couch, Daddy at the other end. Mom was looking through a phone book, and Daddy had his laptop open.

"Emma, dear," Mom said. "Come over here and sit down."

Emma took a deep breath, then went and sat between them. She didn't lean back against the sofa. She sat straight up, as if ready to leap up and run out again.

"Well?" Mom said. "This is a fine mess, isn't it?"

Emma nodded. Even though she wasn't sure whether or not it was a mess. But she knew better than to argue.

Daddy closed his laptop. He turned to Emma. "Have you taken a look at the front hall floor?" he asked.

Emma shook her head.

"Well, I suggest you go look," Daddy said.

"I'll go with her!" McClain said, and she popped up off the floor, dropping Kelley. Kelley meandered over to the window and found a place for herself in a little patch of sunlight.

Emma opened the big wide doors that led into the hall. The sun was shining through the front door window, striking the floor with sparkles of sunlight. The floor was shiny, and the sun gleaming on it made a pretty pattern of colors. It was a parquet floor. That's what Daddy called it—squares of wood nestled up against other squares of wood. It looked a little bit like a puzzle put together in a pretty design.

Emma didn't understand why Mom had called it a fine mess.

And then she saw them: footprints. Dog footprints. They ran down the center of the parquet floor, big and wide. And very, very blue. The footprints ran up to the front door, then turned around and ran back to the family room—and then, if Emma was counting right, back and forth another time. Why? Woof must have had to go to the bathroom really bad.

She bent and scraped at the paint with her fingernail and a tiny bit came off. She scraped again. Another tiny bit came off. It would take a long, long time of scraping before the floor would be clean.

Emma went back in the family room.

"So?" Daddy said.

Emma shrugged. "So, I guess it's a mess, huh?" she said.

"You *guess*?" Mom said. "Do you know how much it will cost to repair that? And that we probably can't get it done before the wedding?"

"Why not?" Emma asked.

"I'll tell you why not," Daddy said. "They have to bring in big machines. They have to sand the floor to remove the paint. And the finish. The sanding puts out a ton of dust. And it will cost two thousand dollars!"

"*Thousand*?" Emma said.

"*Thousand*," Daddy said. "Two thousand. I've been looking up floor refinishers on line, and Mom's been looking them up in the phone book, and they all give the same estimate. More or less."

Emma didn't answer. She felt terrible.

"And," Mom said, "your daddy and I worked so hard to have the house ready for the wedding, with a few days to spare. And now, instead of being able to rest and relax, we've spent all morning online or on the phone. Or at the vet. And why? Because you disobeyed us!"

"I didn't disobey!" Emma said. "You said, 'don't paint your room.' You didn't say anything about my closet."

"Oh?" Mom said. "So we should spell it all out? Don't paint your room, and don't paint the closet, and don't paint the closet doors, and don't paint the bookcases, and by the way, don't paint the windowsills. Is that what you mean?"

"I didn't paint the doors or the windowsills," Emma grumbled. But she was smart enough to say it to herself, not out loud.

"And you almost killed your darling ferret and you let Woof in so he made a mess of everything. It's a good thing the stairs carpet is an Oriental one, with all mixed colors, because, of course, there's paint on that, too, only, fortunately, you can't see it, and . . . "

The twins were clashing their toy cars together. "'Mergency, 'mergency, nine one one!" Ira yelled.

"'Mergency, nine one one!" Lizzie yelled. There was more clashing of cars.

"Tim," Mom said over the racket. "Do you think you could take those two outside? Or maybe up to play in their rooms?"

Tim nodded. "Sure!" he said, and he closed his book. "Come on, you two," he said. He went over to the play garage and gathered up the twins and the garage in his arms. "Let's go play outside."

"Oh, yippee! Will you play with us?" Ira yelled. "In the dirt? Like real cars?"

"In the mud. A car wreck," Lizzie said.

"Sure," Tim said, smiling. "We'll have a good smash-up."

He sent a look to Emma, a secret message, an 'I'm sorry' look. And then he went out with the twins.

The room became quiet. *Too quiet*, Emma thought.

"Why don't you go too, McClain?" Mom said.

McClain shook her head. She moved over and rested her head on Emma's shoulder. "No," McClain said. "I'm sticking with Emma."

Chapter Nineteen
All Better. Sort Of.

That's all it took—Tim's "I'm sorry" look, and McClain sticking with Emma—for Emma to begin to cry. And cry. And cry. And when McClain wrapped her chubby little arms around Emma's middle, Emma thought she might never stop crying.

"It's all right, Emma," Mom said after a minute. "Don't fuss and cry, please."

"Why not?" Emma said. "I've made a mess."

"Okay," Mom said. "You've made a mess. But there's no need to cry about it. It's not the end of the world."

"Want to bet?" Emma sobbed.

She jumped up off the floor. "I'm going to my room!" she said. "To my closet!"

And she ran down the hall, the hall that she had ruined, and up the stairs to her room. She slammed the door and got inside her closet. Her storm closet. Her safe place.

She threw herself on the quilts she had made for her bed and buried her face in the pillow. It did feel safe here. It felt . . . secret. Even though everyone in the family knew about it by now.

After a minute, she heard a tiny knock on her door. She frowned.

"Come in," she called. The door opened. After a minute, McClain came over to the closet, holding Kelley in her arms. Suddenly, Emma wondered: *Was Kelly poisoned too? Was Kelley going to die?*

Emma started to cry again. She'd have to call Dr. Pete and ask if they should take Kelley to see him. Except Kelley had slept with McClain last night. She did every night. So she hadn't been exposed to the paint fumes. And there was no paint on her, except for the blue patch on her back from a few days ago. And even that was fading.

McClain curled up beside Emma on her closet bed.

"I love you," McClain said, throwing her arm over Emma's back.

"Mom and Daddy don't!" Emma cried. "They are so mad at me."

"But they love you. Kelley loves you." McClain put Kelley right in Emma's face. Emma pulled back.

Kelley had really bad breath. Cat-food-fish breath.

There was another knock on the door. Had the whole family finally learned their manners?

Emma didn't answer.

McClain did. "Come in!" she called.

And they did—Mom and Daddy both.

Emma wanted them to go away. Far away.

Mom and Daddy walked into the closet. They sat down, side by side, on Tim's bed.

"Emma?" Daddy said.

"I've ruined everything!" Emma cried. "*Everything*. Just like Mom said. I'm costing you thousands of dollars, and I almost killed Marmaduke, and I ruined your rest days. And now, when the bride, when Annie, walks down the hall, it won't be beautiful anymore. And it should be."

"We'll get a carpet and cover it up," Mom said. "We should have thought of that before. A runner, it's called. I'm sure we can get one by tomorrow."

"But you're supposed to rest tomorrow," Emma sobbed.

"It's all right," Daddy said. He looked at Emma across the few feet that separated the beds. "May I come over and hug you?"

"No," Emma said. Even though she wanted a hug more than anything. But she was such a bad kid!

"Emma," Mom said. "Maybe you can stop crying

123

and tell Daddy and me something. Why did you want to make a closet like this? I don't mean about painting it. I mean, why in here? It's so . . . so hidden."

"That's why," Emma sobbed. "It's my safe place, my place to come when Annie moves away! And it will be safe for Tim too, and . . . "

Both Mom and Daddy were shaking their heads. "Safe?" Daddy said. "Don't you feel safe in this house?"

Emma sucked in her breath. "I do," she said. "But Tim doesn't. Not in thunderstorms. And when Annie goes away, we won't be able to go up to be with her."

"So?" Mom said.

"So," Emma said. "Annie always makes the scary things go away. Like, if she was home right now, I bet she'd make this all better."

"But Emma," Mom said. "Annie's not leaving us. She's family. We've told you that many times. And if she goes to Bo's to live, then she'll still be here in the daytime. Besides, I still don't understand. Why don't you feel safe? With Daddy and me?"

"I do feel safe!" Emma said. "It's just sometimes, I want to feel . . ."

In her mind, she searched for the right word. Comforted? Well, yes. But not that exactly. Understood? Sort of.

She sucked in her breath. She settled on a word—two words. "Protected," she whispered. "Loved."

That's when Daddy lifted Emma up in his arms as if she were no bigger than McClain. He took her over to Tim's bed, and they both sat down beside Mom. Daddy rocked her and hummed to her. When she was little, Daddy would sing to her. Emma didn't remember the name of the song he was singing now, but it was one she remembered from long ago.

"Don't you know, I mean, really, really know, that we love you?" Daddy whispered into her hair. "And we'll always protect you. That's what people do when they love one another. No matter what."

Emma nodded. "Yes. But I mess up so much! None of the other kids do. Like Tim's so good. And McClain, well, she's so cute. And the twins are little, and they don't ever do anything really bad. It's just me who messes up everything! And I never mean to."

"And when you mess up, you think we don't love you any longer?" Mom asked.

Emma nodded. "I think you don't. I mean . . ." She looked at Mom, then at Daddy. "I mean, I wouldn't, if I had a kid like me."

That made Mom laugh. Daddy too. Even Emma began to laugh. McClain started jumping up and down on the bed.

125

"Oh, my dear," Daddy said, rocking Emma again. "I wish you knew how much you are loved. And cherished. And you know what else, Emma? You have very creative ideas."

Emma nodded. "I know," she said. "I mean, sometimes I do."

"You do," Daddy said, hugging Emma again. "Really. Like making a snug place for yourself and your brother. You didn't wait for Annie to move and then worry and fuss. You took on a project. And made it work."

"And messed it up," Emma muttered.

"No," Daddy said. "You didn't mess it up. You messed up the painting, maybe."

"Emma, can I tell you something?" Mom said. She sent a look to Daddy.

He nodded.

"Okay," Mom said. "Daddy and I have been talking about this. You know we'll need a room for New Baby. And it has to be a room of its own. Because, as you know, babies sometimes cry at night. We don't want New Baby to wake up everybody."

Emma nodded. She remembered.

"So maybe New Baby could have this room," Mom said. "And if Annie goes to live with Bo, then you could have Annie's room."

"Oh, I could?!" Emma cried. She sat up, pulling away from Daddy. "Could I really? Oh, I'd love that! I love Annie's apartment."

"Well, you wouldn't have the whole apartment. We're thinking we could turn the big living room up there into a playroom for all you kids. We could get a Ping-Pong table, and other big things you kids would like. But the bedroom would be yours."

"Oh!" Emma cried. "I'd love that. I'd love, love, love it! Oh, thank you so much."

"Well, don't get too excited yet," Daddy said. "Because I have a feeling that Annie and Bo might decide to stay here. And if they do, I bet you can visit them both up there in their apartment. They hinted at that earlier. Bo said he'd enjoy being part of our family, and all the same rules would apply."

"Oh," Emma said. "So . . . so they might stay? Here?"

Daddy nodded. So did Mom.

"Oh," Emma said again.

This was the thing she'd been wanting all along—for Annie to stay, for Bo to stay. And now it seemed it might actually happen.

But darn! She also wanted Annie's bedroom.

Chapter Twenty
Annie's Family Is Here!

It was getting wild and stormy outside, and snow was beginning to spatter against the windows. Wind was chasing itself around the corners of the house.

Emma lay snug in her bed, not her closet bed, her regular one, because she'd found the closet floor bed wasn't nearly as comfortable as her real bed.

It was late, and she pulled the covers up to her chin. She lay there, thinking of Annie and the wedding and the sisters. Annie's sisters and mum were all arriving tonight. Daddy had worried about the weather, because storms could sometimes delay flights. But Daddy had checked the computer, and the flight from Shannon airport in Ireland was right on time. Annie's sisters and her mum would be here. Annie was already here. Bo had gone to Pennsylvania to meet up with his family and drive them back.

Emma's beautiful dress was in her closet, her snug, storm closet. The little kids' new clothes were hanging on the back of Mom's bedroom door—"to keep them safe from small dirty hands," Mom had said. And Annie's wedding dress was on the plane with her mum. Annie's mum had made the dress, using Annie's sister, Bridget, as the model, because Bridget and Annie were the exact same size.

It seemed that everything would be perfect for the wedding.

Even the hall floor was all right. Emma had had a brilliant idea. That afternoon, she'd called Dr. Pete and asked if she could have some of the stuff he'd used on Woof's paws. She even said she'd pay for it.

Dr. Pete just laughed and said there was no charge, and he also said Marmaduke was ready to come home! Emma went and picked up Marmaduke, and also she got the paint remover stuff that was gentle on dogs. When she came home, she cleaned the hall floor while Mom and Daddy made dinner. In an hour, it was done! It was completely clean, and none of the shine had come off, either.

Both Mom and Daddy told her how creative she was and how proud they were of her. And how the floor was beautiful and it wouldn't cost two thousand dollars to fix!

It made Emma think: *She did have good ideas.*

Some of them didn't work out so well. But some did.

It was kind of like all the changes that were happening in her life and in the house. Some might be good. And some not so good. But mostly, they weren't things to worry about because Emma could always fix what wasn't right. That made Emma smile.

Lying in bed and thinking, unable to sleep because of being so excited, Emma began to imagine the wedding and how it would look. It made her wish that she, Emma, could get married too. Not yet, of course, but some day.

It would be fun to be a bride in a pretty dress with a handsome husband. But who would she marry? When she was little, she used to think she would marry Tim. But she knew now that was silly. There was a boy in her class, Jared, whom she liked. But not enough to marry.

And then she fell asleep, dreaming of beautiful wedding dresses and handsome husbands, but it turned out that the handsome husband was Woof who woke Emma up.

Or maybe it was the noise and talk out in the driveway that awakened her. There were squeals of laughter and, and . . .

Emma leaped from her bed.

She looked out her window.

A long, black car was in the driveway—the limo! And a driver was unloading bags. And a bunch of women—girls, Annie's sisters—were there too. And Annie and Mom and Daddy. And there was lots of talking and noise and laughter. Everybody was hugging everybody.

The limo driver was hurrying with the luggage, trying to keep it all dry and away from the snow that was quickly gathering. Daddy went to help him. As Emma watched, snow piled up on the shiny black top of the limo, and the windshield wipers worked furiously to keep the windshield clean.

Then everyone was spilling into the house, still talking and laughing and talking some more. It sounded as if everyone was talking at the same time.

Emma wondered, *Is anyone listening?*

Emma slid her feet into her froggie slippers, grabbed the robe lying on the floor by her bed, threw it on, and pulled the sash tight.

She opened her bedroom door and peered out. Were any of the other kids awake? It didn't seem like they were. Even Tim's door was closed tight.

Emma ran down the stairs and into the family room where everyone had gathered. They were still talking and laughing and hugging each other and also hugging Mom and Daddy. One sister was even on the floor, hugging Woof.

131

The noise stopped when Emma opened the door and stepped in.

One of the sisters put a hand up to her mouth. "A fairy!" she said, turning to Annie. "Oh, a beautiful fairy."

"Truth and it is," said another.

"I've waited my whole life to see one," someone else said.

It was Annie's mum who said that, it had to be. The person, woman, who had spoken was almost as beautiful as Annie and the sisters, although Emma could see she was older. Her clothes weren't as bright and pretty. Her coat was black, and she wore old-lady shoes. Her hair, although long and tied back with a bright ribbon, was gray. She was seated on the sofa, and she held out her arms.

"Are you a fairy?" she asked. "You must be. You are so beautiful."

Emma looked at Annie.

Annie looked back, laughing.

Emma couldn't help it. And she knew it would be all right.

She grinned.

"Are you sure there are fairies?" she asked.

Chapter Twenty-One
Finally All All Right

The day had arrived. The guests had arrived.
The food and flowers had been delivered.
The hour had come. The time for the wedding.

Tim and Daddy helped seat the guests in rows of chairs set up in the family room, folding chairs covered with white cloth with bows in back. They looked like little dresses all lined up. When everyone was seated, the minister gave a signal, and all the guests stood up.

Lizzie walked in first, smiling at everyone as though being in a wedding was something she did every day. Next came Tim and Ira. Ira was holding a small white pillow with the wedding ring on it—pinned so it wouldn't roll away and get lost. Tim would help unpin it when the time came, because Ira couldn't manage safety pins yet. Tim looked very handsome in his suit, as he leaned toward Ira, as if to protect him. Actually, Emma knew Tim was afraid that Ira might scoot away to the backyard to play. But Ira was on his best behavior. Then came McClain. She was on better-than-best behavior, looking as sweet as an angel in her fluffy dress. Even her curls were behaving, not springing all over the place.

And then it was Emma's turn. For some reason, her heart was thumping hard, although she wasn't sure why. It was probably because she was feeling scared and nervous, walking in front of all these people. She was holding a small bunch of flowers in her hand, a bouquet with tiny pink and white roses and baby's breath, all tied with a long white satin ribbon and a bow.

Emma felt pretty. People or Mom were always telling her how beautiful she was, but Emma had never really believed them. But now, today, she did.

And right behind Emma was the prettiest one ever—Annie.

Annie's hair spilled down her back, lying soft and fluffy on her shoulders. Her long white gown had tiny beads all over it, sewn to the skirt like bits of sunshine. There was a small thing that looked like a crown on her head, and from the crown, a white veil fell down and covered her head and face.

Daddy accompanied her to the altar, since Annie's

father had long since gone to heaven. Daddy was wearing one of those dress-up suits that men wear for formal occasions, a blue suit with a fancy white shirt and a funny looking collar. Emma thought he looked very handsome.

Violin music played as Annie walked in. The violinist didn't play "Here Comes the Bride," which Emma thought he should have played. Instead he performed one of Annie's favorite songs, "Amazing Grace."

Bo stood waiting at the altar, watching Annie as she approached. He had slicked down his usually wild hair, and he was wearing the same kind of dress-up suit that Daddy wore.

He looked very handsome too.

When Annie and Daddy got to the front, Emma moved a little to the side so she could see better. She turned and looked at Annie's face.

Mom had moved up too and took Emma's hand.

The violinist continued to play and inside her head, Emma sang the song. She knew the words by heart, since Annie sang it all the time.

Others in the room must have known too, because someone started singing, and then others joined in. Most people just hummed the tune, but a few sang the words.

Amazing grace
How sweet the sound,
That saved a wretch like me.
I once was lost
But now am found.
Was blind,
But now, I see.

Emma liked that song, but she liked one of Annie's others better. The violinist didn't play it, though, so Emma sang it inside her head.

When Irish eyes are smiling.
Sure it's like a morn in spring.
In the lilt of Irish laughter, you can hear the
  angels sing.
When Irish hearts are happy,
All the world seems bright and gay
For when Irish eyes are smiling
Sure it steals your heart away.

Emma knew that Bo had stolen Annie's heart. Annie was in love.

Tears filled Annie's eyes. But Emma knew, she knew for sure, they were happy tears.

And as the wedding progressed, and the minister pronounced them man and wife, and they gave one another a big, long kiss, Emma knew everything was going to be all right. Whatever Annie decided. Wherever she lived.

Everything was going to be all, all right.